Blame It On
TEXAS

Amy Lillard writing as
Amie Louellen

Dedication

To the "aunts" Cindy and Christa. Love you both!

Chapter One

She should have known she'd find him like this.

Shelby looked down at the oil-stained driveway to the denim-clad legs protruding from underneath the ancient Ford. The hem of the jeans was frayed, the worn cowboy boots dusty and with a few stains of their own.

She propped her hands on her hips, doing her best not to tap her foot in irritation. It would do no good. If there was one thing she'd learned in her time as Ritt McCoy's wife, he had his own timetable and to the devil with anyone else's.

"I said, I need to talk to you."

"And I said, just a minute," his muffled voice returned.

Shelby bit back a growl and used the thick packet of papers to fan herself. That was one thing she didn't miss about Texas—the heat. But with any luck and the good Lord's grace, she'd only be here another few minutes, an hour at the most, and then she'd be on her way back to California.

A trickle of sweat ran down between her shoulder blades and into the small of her back. Shelby fanned harder and checked her watch. She'd been waiting twenty minutes for Ritt to finish whatever it was he was doing to the truck and sign on the dotted line. That was nineteen more than she cared to wait.

"Ritt."

"Shelby."

"I need you to sign these."

"In a minute."

"Now. I have a plane to catch."

She jumped back, nearly snapping the heel off one peep-toe pump. They had been a special purchase for this trip along with the form-fitting black dress that hugged her like a second skin. Scrambling to get out of the way, she managed to maintain her balance as Ritt pushed the creeper from under the truck.

And there he was, the boy who stole her heart, took her virginity, and married her all in one summer. Well, he'd had her heart for years before that. And he wasn't a boy any longer; though the years, she grudgingly admitted, had been very kind to him.

"What?" he asked. Even lying down, he looked taller, broader, more. She was glad to have the advantage, standing over him like she was.

"I'm in a hurry."

"Not my problem." He disappeared in a quick swoosh back under the truck. But he left his image behind. Dark blond hair curling from under a ratty Longhorns baseball hat. Dirt smeared T-shirt covering a chest she didn't remember as having quite so many muscles. Long legs, firm lips, square jaw.

"I've flown over a thousand miles to get you to sign these. The least you could do is get out from under there and do it." Her voice rose in pitch, the whine she'd been tamping down rising to the surface. Couldn't he see how they needed this? That it was time to move forward?

There was a loud clunk, which sounded like head versus oil pan, then a muffled curse.

He rolled out again, and before she knew what had happened he was towering over her. She took a couple of steps back for good measure, unable to meet his blue-gold gaze as he studied her face.

"What is it, Shelby? What is so important that you flew all the way out here to grace me with your presence?"

She was wrong. The years had been more than kind to him, they had outright adopted him.

7

Had he always been this tall? This broad? This…masculine?

He had, she decided. But after seven years away, she had forgotten what a man her Texas boy had been.

She licked her lips, the sight of him bringing back more memories than she cared to delve through. Prom night, at the lake after the baseball games, Saturday afternoon in the canyon…

He raised his brows. "I'm waiting."

Waiting? "Oh, the papers," she squeaked. "I need you to sign the divorce papers."

"You flew all the way here for that?" He picked up a rag and started wiping his fingers on it. Shelby could smell the oil on him, the fabric softener in his shirt, and the heat from his body.

"I didn't think you'd sign them any other way."

"You didn't trust me to sign them." He tucked the stained rag into the back pocket of his Levis and adjusted his hat.

"My attorney has sent them twice now."

"I lost a set in the move." He jerked his head toward the house he had lived in his entire life.

Shelby took a deep breath, doing her best to formulate her most persuasive offense. "No problem. I happen to have a set right here." She pulled the papers from the manila envelope and flattened them against the hood of the truck. They ruffled in the breeze as she dug around in her purse. "And here's a pen." She handed it to him triumphantly. She was minutes away from being a free woman. Free of Ritt McCoy and free to move forward.

"Sign, please." Her words came out confident and true. There wasn't a waver in her voice, no sign that being this close to him had her tied in knots. He could always do that to her. They brought out the worst in each other. A divorce was for the best.

"I haven't had a chance to look over them yet."

"My attorney sent them to you last month."

He shrugged.

"I need you to sign—"

"I think I should have a chance to read them—"

"I flew all the way out here—"

"I mean it's only fair—"

"Fair?"

"No one told you to come out here."

When had he stepped so close?

"Sorry you had to dirty your precious bohemian feet to come to mean old Texas. But I ain't signin'."

Shelby took another deep breath. "Why are you being so stubborn?"

He glared at her.

"What do you want, Ritt? A signing bonus?" Oops. Wrong thing to say.

His eyes narrowed, his jaw ground together, and that good ol' boy look froze on his face. "Funny thing you should mention that, sugar. 'Cuz that may be the only thing that'll get me to sign." He turned on his heel and stalked to the porch. "Come on, Clyde."

A fat basset hound stood and stretched and followed behind his master. Without a backward glance, Ritt jerked open the door, then he and the dog disappeared into the house.

The wind blew the papers onto the desert-hot driveway.

Shelby bent to pick them up, crazy nostalgia nearly choking her. She should have known that seeing him again after so long was a bad idea. She should have known that he wouldn't make it easy for her. But she hadn't thought her own emotions would get in her way. This is what she wanted. What she needed. She bit her lip and stared at the front door of the house.

She'd give him a few minutes, then she'd try again. She had plenty of time before she had to get back to the airport. Plenty of time to convince him to sign. Well, it would help if she knew *why* he wouldn't sign. It wasn't like they had a real marriage. They'd only lived together a couple of months. A couple of passionate, turbulent months.

Shelby pushed those memories back and started toward the house. What was done was done. She had gotten pregnant, gotten married, and lost the baby. After that, the trouble began. Then her mother met a man from California, and they were off again.

She picked her way across the cobbled walk to the house. Nostalgia hit her again as she stepped onto the porch. How many times had she sat there with Ritt, watching the sun set, drinking lemonade, making out?

She knocked on the door, pulling her composure around her like a cloak. "Ritt. Ritt?"

A grunt sounded from the other side of the green painted wood.

"There's nothing to look over. It's a standard, run-of-the-mill divorce. It says we have irreconcilable differences, and we need to part ways."

"Too busy to deal with this right now."

She stepped to the large bay window and peered inside. Ritt sat on the couch, his feet propped up on the magazine-strewn coffee table. He had a beer in one hand.

"You're not busy." She resisted the urge to growl at him.

He took a drink of his beer then pulled his hat over his eyes as if gearing up for a nap. "Come back tomorrow, Shel. Maybe I can look at them then."

Tomorrow? She didn't have until tomorrow. She needed this done now. The sooner she had the papers signed, the sooner she could start her new, very respectable life. Well, technically she had started her new life, but it was hard to fully embrace the changes with her failed marriage hanging around her neck like an old dead goose.

"Ritt." She tapped on the glass, but he didn't move.

Dang it! Dang his stubborn hide.

She raised her hand to rap on the glass again but lowered it instead. Now was not the time to be demanding. Not when he held all the cards.

"I'm leaving a set out here. I expect you'll find time to look them over." *Despite your busy schedule.* Her mouth twisted in annoyance. She set the papers on the wooden church pew next to the door and anchored them with a terra cotta pot filled with wilting impatiens. "I'll see you tomorrow." She managed not to choke on the words, then she turned on her heel and retreated to the rental car.

She'd simply have to go into town and get a hotel room. With any luck, by tomorrow afternoon, she'd be divorced.

****

Whoever said the line about the plans of mice and men was one smart cookie, but that didn't help the situation any. By the time Shelby had driven into Amarillo, called the airlines to change her ticket, and left a message at her bakery that she wasn't coming home until tomorrow she still had hours to kill. The temptation to drive back to Randall and walk around, see how much things had changed, and how much they had stayed the same was so strong she almost took her car keys and locked them in the hotel safe. Now was not the time for reminiscing. It was the time to move forward.

Instead, she watched reruns of *Friends* and ate pretzels from the honor bar. It was no big, she told herself. If Ritt wanted to control this situation she would let him. If that made him feel better, then she could play the game to get what she wanted. Tomorrow she would go back to his house and get him to sign the papers, and that would be the end of that. She would be able to truly start over. Free from Ritt, free from the past. A brand new start...that was exactly what she needed. She mentally dusted her hands of the situation and drifted off to sleep.

****

The next morning, Shelby re-donned her dress, pulling it over the underwear she had

13

thankfully remembered to rinse out in the sink the night before.

She'd bought a toothbrush and toothpaste from the vending machine in the lobby, so her teeth were clean. She pulled her hair back into a ponytail in lieu of washing it and scrubbed her body with the hotel-provided soap. Not luxurious by any stretch, but she was clean and ready to face Ritt.

Except he wasn't at home when she pulled the rental in front of his parents' house. She drove to the convenience store on the corner. Of course the young clerk there knew Ritt by name, but he hadn't seen him all morning.

Shelby got back into her car, her only option driving around town until she spotted his truck. It had cost her a whopping three hundred dollars to change to an open-ended plane ticket, so she had the time. Now if she could only find the patience.

Thankfully Randall was the typical one-horse town and fifteen minutes later she spotted the rusted blue Ford in front of the bait shop. Leave it to Ritt to pick now to go fishing. Well, he could just postpone his little trip until she got her signatures. After that, she didn't give a flip what he did.

She parked the rental in front of the tiny building, shoved it into park, then took a deep breath. *Almost over.* Her heart gave a painful thump. Stupid nostalgia. That was all it was. She grabbed the manila envelope and walked toward the shop door.

The interior was cool and dark and smelled like dirt. It shouldn't have comforted her nerves, but it did. Suddenly she remembered all the times that she and Ritt had come here before heading out to the lake to fish. Well, they usually ended up dropping a line in the water then making out all afternoon, but fishing had been their original intent. She wondered who he was fishing with these days.

She pushed her sunglasses on her head and blinked to adjust to the dim shop.

"Shelby? Shelby Patterson? Is that you?"

She blinked once again and brought the man into focus. "Craig!" She threw her arms around his neck and hugged him tight. "I haven't seen you in—"

"Seven years," came the dry voice behind the counter.

Shelby released Craig and coolly eyed her soon-to-be ex. Ritt stood with his rear propped on the back counter. He had a bottle of Dr. Pepper in one hand, peanuts floating around the top. Same old Ritt. He wore a bright yellow T-shirt that said, "The Master-Baiter" and a pair of disreputable jeans. A barbed wire tattoo peeked out from under the hem on one bicep. That was new.

15

So Ritt worked at the bait shop. Showed what a bullet she'd dodged. He'd never had any drive other than baseball. Why he never went pro was a mystery for the ages. And yet one more reason he had to sign. Her bakery was hers. She had worked hard to build her reputation from nothing. There was no way she would let Ritt swoop in and take half of all that she had worked so hard to create.

"It's tomorrow," she said, wishing she could stay and visit with Craig. It had been so long since she'd seen him. Since that day she and her mother packed everything in the back of their Volkswagen and headed for California. That day Craig had asked her to stay for Ritt's sake, had told her that Ritt loved her. She'd replied that if it were the truth he would come after her. He never did.

"I'm busy." He took a swig of the soda then idly chewed on the peanuts.

"Surely you found time to look over them last night."

"I did. And stop calling me Shirley."

She ignored his joke and pulled her copy of the papers out of their envelope. "Then all you need to do is sign."

He shook his head. "I need to have my attorney look over them. There were a couple of places—"

"Ritter McCoy." Shelby braced her hands on her hips. "You are making this much harder than it has to be."

He shrugged.

"What's going on here?" Craig looked from one of them to the other.

"Oh, a little bit of unfinished business," Shelby said. Why wouldn't he just sign? It might be silly of her but the longer she had to wait, the more worried she became that she'd be stuck in Texas forever.

Craig glanced toward Ritt. "What kind of papers?"

"Divorce papers," her husband said.

"You've never gotten a divorce?"

Ritt shook his head.

"Are you serious?"

Ritt shrugged again, and Shelby was certain she hated the motion. "It never came up."

She turned her attention to Craig. Maybe he could help her get Ritt to sign. Was it such a hard thing to do? "But now that it has, Ritt is being a little...hesitant." She held out the papers toward her almost ex-husband, but he didn't budge.

"I said I need my attorney to take a look at them."

"I *am* your attorney." Craig took the papers from Shelby.

"Let me look these over. I'll get back to you by tomorrow afternoon."

"Tomorrow?"

"Sorry, I'm booked all day."

"Tasting cake," Ritt interjected.

"Last tux fitting."

Tux? Cake? "You're getting married?"

Craig nodded. "This weekend."

"That's terrific. Anyone I know?"

"Delilah."

"Simpson?" They were only now getting around to tying the knot?

"Simpson-Jones."

"Oh." Shelby nodded. There had been a running pool over who would get married first. She and Ritt or Craig and Delilah. How ironic that Craig and his high school sweetheart were finally getting married when she and Ritt were finally getting divorced.

"If you're still around this weekend, we'd love for you to come."

"If I'm still here," she mumbled. She wanted as far away from Randall as quickly as possible, though it would be nice to see her two long-ago friends finally find happiness.

"Swing by my office tomorrow afternoon." He handed her a business card. "Say about three?"

Shelby nodded reluctantly. What choice did she have? She'd book the hotel room for one more night. And call the bakery again. They would have to make do without her. One more day in Texas was worth the freedom at the end.

"And you—" Craig pointed to Ritt. "I'll see you at two at Harris's."

****

Ritt hated the mall. But he had promised Craig, and he kept his promises. Unlike some people he knew.

Visions of long, tanned legs flitted through his mind, and he pushed them away. After all these years, Shelby wanted a divorce.

He strolled into the bridal shop and tried not to itch. These places gave him the heebie-jeebies.

Long white dresses that looked like they were made from moonbeams and stars. They were nothing but expectations, and unrealistic ones at that. Look at him and Shel. They should have made it, but too many things had been stacked against them.

He walked to the counter and gave the black-clad attendant his name. In minutes he was in a dressing room, trying on his best man's tux.

How he hated these things. Why couldn't people just get married? Why did it have to include all the hype and drama? It only made it hurt all the more when it ended.

19

He shook away the negative thought. Craig and Delilah would make it. They were older now. They had gotten their problems out of the way. The big ones anyway. School, family. Delilah had even married someone else; though Ritt thought she only did it to get back at Craig for focusing on his education instead of her. He pulled a face. Women.

Ritt stepped from the dressing room and headed for the three-way mirrors with the small risers in front.

Craig was already there.

"You clean up nice, bait man."

Ritt shot him a look. "Let's get this over with."

The seamstresses bustled around, making marks here and there to fit the tux. Jacket shoulders, arm lengths, hems. Ritt stood as patiently as possible when he really wanted to run and duck for cover. Seeing Shelby again had been like a knife to the heart. Everything he had wanted, everything he hadn't gotten in his life all rolled up into one.

"So Shelby's back."

Ritt snorted. "For a day."

"She said she'd come to the wedding."

Ritt shrugged.

The seamstress frowned and pulled on the shoulders of his jacket.

"Sorry," Ritt murmured.

"You know you don't have to make this so difficult." Craig's voice was patient and understanding. But how could he know what Ritt was feeling?

"Why should I make this easy on her?"

"Well, you love her for one."

Ritt stifled a snort. "That was a long time ago, buddy."

"Then let her go. She's made good for herself, you know."

"How do you know?"

"Facebook."

"That's just what she needs." Respectability. That was the one thing that Shelby cared most about. With a mother like hers, who could blame her?

"She owns a bakery. Cupcakes and designer cakes. That kind of thing."

"Shelby?" he scoffed. "Shelby Patterson?"

"Shelby McCoy," Craig corrected.

Ritt shook his head. "Shelby can't cook."

"Evidently she learned."

"You know this how?"

"Google. You really got to get out more."

"So that's how you spent the afternoon, googling my wife?"

Craig made a face. "That sounds dirty, but yeah… And looking over the papers."

"You told her that you couldn't get to them till tomorrow."

"You know I'm going to have to draw up new ones."

Ritt nodded. "I suppose."

The seamstress tugged on his hem one last time. "All done, sir."

Ritt turned to look at himself in the mirror. Monkey suit. Pomp and circumstance. All this wedding jive. Yet he couldn't help but wonder if he'd done all this for Shelby maybe she would have stayed.

No, the voice inside him whispered. They were doomed from the beginning. An unplanned pregnancy was the bottom of the respectability barrel. There was no getting out of that one. He shouldn't have been surprised when she ran. But that didn't make it hurt any less.

Chapter Two

Promptly at three the next afternoon, Shelby entered the offices of Coltrane, Elliot, and Johnson. They had a cool and breezy look, like a slice of the Caribbean had been brought to the Texas panhandle. Pale, aqua-tinted walls, crisp white trim and large potted plants. Only the golden-toned wood floors added a touch of the real locale.

A small brunette sat behind a large desk, her breezy white outfit in perfect harmony with her surroundings.

"Shelby Patterson. I'm here to see Craig Combs."

The receptionist smiled and scanned her appointment calendar. "I have a Shelby McCoy."

How long had it been since someone had called her that? Seven years if a day. She'd never really gone by Ritt's name. There hadn't been any time. But using Patterson had taken away some of the sting and made the biggest mistake of her life seem like…less.

"McCoy is my married name."

The woman raised one dark brow in question. "Second door on the left. Go on back. They're expecting you."

Shelby nodded, her heart pounding in her chest. It was all about to end.

Craig was seated behind a large, dark-wood desk. A computer monitor flashed in front of him, a familiar envelope lying open on the large calendar/blotter.

Ritt slouched in one of the leather chairs facing the desk, his booted feet stretched out in front.

Shelby stopped short. Her breath caught in her throat. A hand fluttered to her hair to smooth down her tidy chignon. She was grateful she had taken the time to buy a new shirt and skirt for the occasion. She had been tempted to pick up a tracksuit at Penney's to see her through, but instead had splurged on a short gray skirt and a silky white button-down from Dillard's. It seemed like today she was going to need all the confidence she could muster.

"What are you doing here?" she blurted.

Ritt rolled his head in her direction, the brim of that stupid orange baseball hat hiding his eyes. "It's my divorce too."

"There was no need…" Her words trailed off as Craig stood.

He smoothed a hand over the front of his shirt and tie as he motioned with the other for her to sit. "Glad you could make it, Shelby."

She nodded, then cautiously picked her way around to the front of the chair. She had to step over Ritt's feet to do so, and she wondered if he'd positioned himself that way to make it difficult for her. She wouldn't put it past him. It seemed he had no desire to let things happen smoothly. He hadn't been so opposed that one night down by the lake...

She wiped that thought from her mind, setting her handbag on the floor next to her chair and giving Craig a respectful and attentive look. It beat the heck out of staring at Ritt's biceps. Even out of the corner of her eye she could see the ripped muscles as he sat with his shoulders hunched, his arms crossed over that so broad chest.

"You both know why we're here. Now, in light of other circumstances, there are a few things we need to discuss before getting down to the business of signing."

"What? He hasn't signed them?" Shelby was on her feet in a heartbeat.

"Shelby, there's more to talk about than—"

"Why hasn't he signed them?" Her temper would get her nowhere, but she was two days off already. She wasn't about to spend any more time in Texas than absolutely necessary.

"I'm right here. You can talk to me, you know."

She kept her eyes trained on Craig. "I came here to pick up the papers. Which meant they should be signed. I don't understand why they're not signed."

"See what I mean?" Ritt started. "I told you she was going to be like this."

She rounded on him. "Like what?"

"Guys—" Craig interjected.

"A brat."

"I am not a brat." She stamped her foot to prove it.

"I knew you'd come flying in here, guns blazing, if you didn't get your way."

"Guys, really—"

"What's that supposed to mean?"

"What do you think it means?"

"I don't know. You tell me."

"Guys—"

"I know how you are."

"You don't know me anymore."

"I know this: You're a coward. Come down here demanding a divorce after seven years. You didn't give us a chance. Ever. First sign of trouble and you were out the door. Just took the money and ran. You're running still."

"Both of you shut up!" Craig's command rattled the windows.

Shelby took a deep breath. Ritt was wrong. She wasn't running. She was beginning. She could only do that with an end to her Texas life. That started and ended with her husband.

Funny, but she hadn't thought about him that way in a long time. Not since those first days filled with hope as bright as the sun. Those days were gone forever. Now he was merely someone she'd once known, someone she'd almost had a baby with.

"Sit down, Shelby." Craig's words sounded like he was talking to a pet, but she did as he asked. She wasn't getting anywhere with Ritt like this.

As the thought crossed her mind, he stood. "You know what? I'm outta here."

"Ritt." Craig's voice was low with warning.

"I don't have to sign. Maybe tomorrow, maybe not."

She watched speechless as he walked out the door. That was so like Ritt. He accused her of running, but who was the coward now?

The paneled oak slammed behind him, and Shelby turned back to Craig.

"I'll talk to him," he said.

She pressed her lips together and nodded. What else could she do?

27

Craig picked up the thick packet of papers that held her dreams, her do-over. "Would you like to take a look at these?"

She forced a smile. "Not right now." Her head was starting to pound, her thoughts chasing themselves around in circles. Maybe tomorrow he'd said, which meant another night at the hotel. She'd have to call the shop and tell Kathryn that she'd be out for a couple more days. Luckily she didn't have anything waiting for her attention. There was the Anderson's birthday party this weekend, but Kat could handle that one by herself. The Riley wedding was still two weeks away. Plenty of time to finish that when she got home.

Craig slid the papers into the manila envelope and pushed it across the desk. "You can look over them later."

Shelby nodded. "Why is he—?" She didn't finish. Why was he acting like this? Why was he being so stubborn?

"Your leaving really hurt him, Shelby."

"He didn't even know I was gone."

Craig shook his head. "He knew all right. He lost everything when he lost you and the baby."

It had been seven years. It shouldn't hurt so much when someone mentioned the baby that she and Ritt had made and lost. Yet it did. Some pains never eased.

As bad as it hurt to admit it, losing the baby had been a blessing in disguise, the twist of fate they needed. Without a baby and a wife, Ritt could play ball for Texas. Shelby's grades weren't bad, but not good enough to get her into the university. Her mother didn't have the money to put her through college. What choice did Shelby have but to move to California? She was going to be left behind anyway. He'd be leaving. Her mother was leaving. What did Ritt expect her to do? Stay living with his parents?

She shook her head. "I left so he could go back to school."

"He'd already lost his place on the team."

"But—" Her mother had told her it was for the best. They would leave, get a fresh start. Ritt would go to school, play baseball for Texas University like had been his dream since as long as she could remember, then everybody would be happy again.

What did you think? That he'd graduated with a degree in engineering and that's why he works at the bait shop?

"You know Ritt." Craig's words brought her out of her thoughts.

She thought she had. Once upon a time.

"He loved you more than anything in the world. Then you left without giving your marriage a chance."

"But the baby—"

Craig shook his head. "The baby wasn't the issue, Shelby. He wanted you. And you walked out."

****

What a day.

Ritt let himself in the house, not bothering to turn on any lights. The remaining rays from a brilliant West Texas sunset were enough for him to get into the house and toe off his boots. Right now all he wanted was to have a beer, check the scores, and forget today ever happened.

He padded to the fridge in his sock feet, opening the door and regarding his options.

"Honey? Is that you?"

If that same voice hadn't filled his dreams for more years than he cared to remember, he might have jumped out of his skin. As it was, he peered around the door.

"Shelby?"

She stood in the archway that led to the dining room. She had on the same shirt and skirt that she'd worn to their meeting with Craig, the same sexy shoes, and one of his mother's gawd-awful floral-print aprons looped over her neck and tied around her waist. She smiled as if she had a secret—a really evil secret—and Ritt felt a shudder skitter down his spine.

"What are you doing here?" It took everything he had not to snarl the words. He wasn't about to let her see how much her presence affected him.

"Is this what I should expect every night?"

Ritt snatched a beer, straightened, then shut the refrigerator door. He popped the top off the brown bottle with the church key mounted on the side of the cabinet and took a healthy swig before answering. "I'm going with no."

"So you don't come home and have a drink before dinner?"

"How'd you get in here?"

"You know, you should really tell your mama to move the spare key. Seven years, Ritt, and it was still there. Speaking of, where are your folks?"

Suddenly the sophisticated baker from this afternoon was replaced by a Texas girl in really high heels.

Damn, she was hot. Right now she was making his blood boil, but for all the wrong reasons.

"They're touring the lower forty-eight in an RV."

She faltered. "They're not here?"

"Nope."

"Kyle?" She seemed hopeful.

"He's in Lubbock."

"So…we're…alone?"

He gave a quick nod.

"Oh." That didn't seem to be part of her plan. The light in her pale gray eyes dimmed a tad before she covered the reaction. "Well, then more for us, right?"

"More what?" He wasn't sure he wanted to know.

"Supper, silly. Why else would I be here?"

"Funny, I was asking myself the same thing." For the first time he noticed the smell coming from the dining room. And all the dirty dishes piled in the sink. And the splatters on the stove. It hadn't looked like this when he left this morning. Mainly because he never cooked, preferring to stop by the diner to eat. Or drive into Amarillo if he wanted something different. Cooking for one was a hassle, a complete waste of time. "You cooked?"

She nodded, a strand of hair working loose from her librarian hairdo to brush against her cheek. "Of course, I did."

"Of course." He took another swig of the beer, wishing instead for something stronger. Anything to dull the longing now pounding through his blood.

She tilted her head to one side, that evil smile back on her face. Well, the smile itself wasn't particularly evil, but it was too innocent to be anything else. What was she up to now?

"Isn't that the job of a good wife?" she said the last two words around an exaggerated pout. "Cook for her husband?"

"Among other things." He watched her carefully molded features. She gave nothing away at his insinuation, but she had to be thinking the same thing. All the times they'd made love, fumbling at first then learning the other's likes and desires, all the secret places. He wondered if he kissed her on that throbbing vein in her neck if she'd sigh like she used to.

"Well, I figured that if you were having such a time signing those papers that maybe you really wanted a wife. So I said to myself, 'Shelby, you must get over there and do everything in your power to be a good wife to your husband.'" Her voice held an inflated Texas drawl.

"Everything?"

Her look was coy, her words a purr. "I made dinner."

Shelby had never been able to cook before, burning everything from eggs to pasta. But her culinary talents were not the reason he'd married her.

Still, what harm could it do to allow her to finish this little charade? What did she think? That she could cook him a little something, and he'd be so grateful that he'd sign her stupid papers? Not likely. But he'd get a free meal out of the deal. He smiled to himself.

This was a game he'd have to see through till the end. Or maybe until he got bored.

Why not let her grovel a little, cook and such, in her efforts to convince him to what? To let her go?

That wasn't something he was ready to do. He was still angry. Still seething over the fact that she'd left. She'd taken his parents' bribe and walked away without a backward glance. He'd given up everything for her and in the end he'd lost it all. So no, he wasn't going to just sign the papers and give her a quickie divorce. She was going to have to work for it.

But there was no reason why he couldn't benefit from this. No siree, none at all.

****

Except Shelby's cooking skills hadn't improved one iota in the seven years they had been estranged.

Ritt dragged his fork through the casserole. At least he thought it was a casserole. How did a person overcook the pasta and undercook the meat in the same dish?

"I thought Craig said you baked cakes or something for a living." Sounded like a scam to him.

"I do."

He looked down at the congealed mess that was, in her terms, "supper" then back up to those unbelievable gray eyes.

"Is your dinner not to your liking?"

"I think I've had enough for one night." He tossed his napkin on the table and stood.

She sat there, innocently picking through her cooked-to-mush mixed vegetables as if searching for lost treasure.

"Come on, Shelby. Time to go."

"Go where?"

"Your hotel."

"But you said I never gave our marriage a chance. How can I do that if I'm staying in a hotel? Besides, there's some big convention and a huge wedding that have all of the rooms from here to Midland booked."

"What are you saying?"

"I'm saying, my dear husband, that I'm moving in."

Chapter Three

Moving in. Ritt scoffed. Moved in was more like it. She already had all of her things scattered throughout the house like she'd been there forever. Toothbrush in the holder next to his, makeup all over the counter, hell, she'd even stashed a box of tampons under the sink.

She was just doing this to get under his skin. So far it was working, but he'd be damned before he'd let her know that.

Ritt punched his pillow into submission. It was impossible to sleep, knowing that she was in the rarely used guest room...so close. Short of twisting her arm behind her back and forcibly kicking her out the door, he had no way of making her leave. Now his best course of action was to pretend that she wasn't there. That she wasn't slowly driving him out of his mind.

"Ritt? Are you asleep?"

He propped himself onto his elbows. What was she, like a ninja or something? He hadn't heard her walk across the creaky old hardwood floors, hadn't heard her open the door to his room, but there she was, backlit from the light he left on in the hallway bathroom. Her silhouette was enticing and doing terrible things to his resolve.

"What now, Shelby?"

"I—" She took two steps into the room, close enough he could smell her designer perfume and the hotel-provided shampoo. "I can't sleep."

"That makes two of us." He hadn't meant to say the words out loud.

He held his breath as she came nearer, finally perching on the edge of the bed. Memories swamped him, those first days living in the garage apartment. Too bad it wasn't livable still, he could have moved out there and let her take over the house until she was tired of this game. As it was now, he'd have to see it through till the end.

Having her this close was torture. He only had to reach out and he could touch her, smooth her hair back from her face, run his fingers down her cheek. How many nights had he prayed to have her back? To have one more chance with her? "I was wondering— " she started.

This wasn't a second chance. Once he signed those papers, she'd be gone in a flash. This was only a delay of game.

"If you wanted to—" She reached out, laid her hand on his arm, the warmth of her fingers burning him with desire.

Just sign, his rational side demanded. Sign and get it over with. Postponing the inevitable wasn't productive. She wanted a life without him; there wasn't much he could do to change that.

"—play cards or something."

Or something came to mind. "Go to bed, Shelby." He turned away, flopping onto his opposite side and willing his breathing to normal, steady and even. He couldn't let her know how her presence affected him.

A heartbeat later he felt the side of the bed sag under her weight.

"What the hell?"

She hoisted herself over him, straddling him for the merest of moments before pushing herself to the other side of the bed.

He could only stare as she wriggled under the covers, burrowing down and making herself totally comfortable. She heaved a contented sigh then closed her eyes.

"Uh, Shelby?"

"Mm-hmmm."

"What are you doing?"

"Sleeping, silly."

If she called him silly one more time he was going to toss her out on her pretty behind.

"This is my bed."

"Uh-huh."

"You are sleeping in the guest room."

"It's lonely in there."

"Too bad."

"Plus Clyde is taking up all the room."

Yay for Clyde. Ritt knew the hound was smart, but he'd never pegged him for desperate.

"It seems silly for me to sleep in there. I mean, we are married."

Bingo. That's what this was all about. Of course. She wanted the papers signed, and she was willing to do whatever it took to get his signature. Even if it meant invading his bed.

Not going to work, sister. He'd sign 'em when he was good and damn ready.

And he wasn't going to be chased out of his bed in the middle of the night by his wife.

He cautiously turned to his other side, careful not to brush against her in the move.

And he'd thought having her in the other room was torture. Next to him he could hear her breathing, feel her warmth, inhale the sweet scent of woman.

Hell. That was the word. Lying next to her was hell.

She murmured in her sleep, the unintelligible syllables smooth like butter against this libido.

He couldn't take this. Not one second more.

With a growl of frustration and a curse under his breath, he threw back the covers and marched into the living room.

Clyde lifted his head when Ritt stomped in. So much for not letting her chase him from his bed. But he couldn't sleep with his wife, and he couldn't very well sleep in his parents' room. She'd already contaminated the sheets with her alluring scent. That left the twin beds in Kyle's room or the sofa. Well, he'd just as soon take his chances with Clyde.

Ritt pushed the lethargic dog to the end of the sofa. Sharing the couch with the hound would be a damned sight easier than sharing the bed with his wife.

Ritt settled down next to his dog and prayed for the morning to come quickly.

****

The smell of burnt woke him. Well, that and the sound of every skillet in the house being banged together.

Ritt resisted the urge to cover his head with the lace-trimmed throw pillow and instead opened one eye to survey the damage to his kitchen. From his vantage point, he could only see Shelby from the side. She was wearing a pair of jeans, obviously new judging from their dark

40

look, a peach colored T-shirt and that damned floral apron from last night.

That same apron had a starring role in his dreams, covering his naked wife who fed him cupcakes while the dog watched and waited for crumbs. He sat up and scratched Clyde behind the ears in apology.

"You're awake." A smile stretched across her face, and Ritt forgot to breathe. Could it be that she was even more beautiful today than she had been when she'd stomped on his heart and left town without a backward glance? Or maybe it wasn't merely beauty, but that mature look of confidence that sucked him in like a vortex.

That was it. Her hair was the same, black-coffee brown, her limbs long and tanned. She still had those killer gray eyes and a smile that could launch ships, even white teeth and that slight indentation in her chin.

But she carried herself like a woman, shoulders back, head up and eyes straight ahead. She hadn't been like that back then. The confidence was intoxicating.

"Oops!"

Ritt jumped to his feet as whatever she was cooking on the stovetop burst into flames. The smoke alarm blared an ear-splitting screech as Clyde let out a howl.

"Oh. My. God." Shelby waved at the small fire with a dishtowel only fanning the flames.

Ritt grabbed the fire extinguisher from under the sink and in seconds the fire was out, the stove, frying pan and its contents coated in frothy white foam.

One good whack with the broom and the smoke detector was silenced.

The hound continued his mournful song.

"Clyde. Clyde!"

The dog stopped yowling and studied them with his sad, basset eyes.

"Enough." Ritt glared at the animal.

Clyde dropped to his belly and laid his chin on his paws.

"Wow. Thanks, Ritt."

He rounded on his wife. "What in the hell do you think you're doing?"

She blinked, then took a step back as if he were about to pounce on her.

Truth was, he might. But not in a good way. It was one thing to have her barge back into his life and another to have her setting fire to his kitchen.

"I only wanted to cook you some breakfast."

"Don't."

"But—" Tears welled in her eyes, and Ritt immediately regretted his tone of voice. Whatever plan she had up her sleeve, fire wasn't

42

part of it. "Isn't that what you wanted? A chance?"

"What are you talking about?"

She swiped at her tears with the back of her hand, smearing her mascara under her eyes. The look should have been ugly, but it made them appear bigger, smoky gray.

"Yesterday in Craig's office. You said I never gave us a chance."

So that's what this is all about. "Don't you think it's a little late for that?"

"We can't go back in time."

He snorted. If only he could…

"Why are you so angry, Ritt?"

"You're kidding, right?"

She pushed herself onto one of the barstools surrounding the kitchen island and propped her heels on the top rung. "No."

This was not the conversation he wanted to have at eight in the morning. Come to think of it, he didn't want to have the conversation at all.

He heaved a sigh and shoved his hands into the front pockets of his jeans. "It was the money, Shel."

She blinked. Then she blinked again as if trying to process his words. "What are you talking about?"

Did she really want to play it like this? All innocence and big eyes. "The money my parents gave your mother to take you away."

He had to hand it to her, the look of disbelief could have won an Oscar. But it only made him madder.

"What money?"

"This has gone on long enough, Shelby. I'm going to take a shower, and when I come back, I expect this mess to be cleaned up."

He turned on his heel and stalked down the hallway, her look of incomprehension trailing behind him.

****

Shelby watched his tight rear disappear down the hall. The sight of it was almost enough to make her forget his words. But not quite.

What money? There was no money. Her mother told her that if they left, Ritt would be able to reclaim his scholarship and go to school that fall. Shelby had agreed to go because she loved him enough to want that for him. She loved watching him play baseball. Loved the light in his eyes when he caught sight of the diamond. Baseball meant everything to him, and she didn't want to be the one who took it all away.

She rinsed out the dishrag and attacked the mess on the stove. At the rate she was going, he would kick her out by nightfall and without signed divorce papers—the one thing she needed most.

She was almost done with the cleanup when Ritt sauntered back into the kitchen. His wet hair was nearly brown, the ends curling softly against his neck. He wore jeans and a T-shirt, which seemed to be his standard fair, this one a tribute to the city of Austin.

He opened the fridge, rummaging around until he found an egg and cold piece of sausage.

She bit her lip, watching as he cracked the egg against the counter top and peeled the shell onto a paper towel.

"What money are you talking about?" she asked.

He sprinkled salt on the boiled egg and took a bite. "Really? You're going to play dumb?"

"I'm not playing." That didn't come out exactly as she'd planned. "I mean, I don't know what you're talking about."

He sighed and retrieved a half-gallon jug of orange juice from the fridge. She tried not to cringe as he drank from the container. He was just trying to make her crazy. "The money my parents…" he said slowly as if that would somehow help her to understand, "…gave your mother." Another long pause. "To take you to California."

"There was no money."

45

"I'm done with this conversation, Shelby. When I get home, I expect your things gone."

"You can't accuse my mother of bribery, and then just…leave."

"I'm not accusing your mother of anything. She was the bribe-ee."

Shelby crossed her arms over her midriff. "That's ridiculous."

"I'm sorry; I don't know what you call someone who takes a bribe."

"My mother would never do that." But even as she said the words, Shelby thought back to those few weeks after the miscarriage. Her hormones had been all wacky, dropping so quickly when there was no longer a baby to support. She had never questioned what her mother had said, that she had met someone from California.

"The money came from my mother's boyfriend."

"The one she went to California to meet, but never materialized."

That was the one. Shelby shook back her hair, not wanting to accept the truth. "That can't be it."

Ritt strolled to the living room desk and plucked the cordless phone from the charger. "Call her."

"What?"

"Call your mom and ask her."

"But—"

"You don't want to know the truth?"

Shelby's stomach cramped painfully. Most probably from eating her own cooking and not from dread. She took the phone. "Fine. I'll call. But when she tells me there was no money, you owe me an apology. And you have to sign the papers."

"She tells you there was no money, then she's a liar."

Shelby decided not to respond. Arguing with Ritt was a useless endeavor. Instead, she dialed her mother's number and tried not to look too smug as she listened to the ring on the other end. Finally the voicemail picked up. "Mom. Hey, I'm here with Ritt, and he's saying that his parents paid you to take me to California. I need you to call me back at this number and tell me that it's not true, 'kay? Thanks. Love you."

"How very unbiased of you." Ritt picked up a piece of the charred bacon and turned it over as if it would be edible upon closer examination.

Shelby shrugged. "What do you care?"

Ritt tossed the bacon in the trash. "Come on, baker. Let's go get some breakfast."

****

Typical Ritt, he took her to breakfast at Cindy's Donut Shop. Shelby was sure she gained ten pounds by just walking in the door. How many times had she and Ritt sat in these same cracked orange booths and ate donut holes until they were about to pop? Too many to count. The crisp fall days before school, the blistering summer days before heading out to fish or work or play around the canyon.

Shelby tamped down those memories and did her best not to keep a running tally of carb intake as Ritt ordered a box of donut holes, two coffees and chocolate milk. How did he stay so...fit and eat like this?

One more day, she told herself as she bit into the fattening confection. Her mother would call back today, tonight at the latest. Once she told Ritt that his parents had not paid her to take Shelby to California, he'd have no reason not to sign the papers, and Shelby would be on her way back home.

"Shelby?"

She turned as a dark-haired pixie approached. Same red lipstick and amber-colored eyes. She'd have known her anywhere. "Delilah?"

Shelby stood and gave her longtime friend a one-armed hug.

"Craig told me he saw you. I was so excited. Please tell me you'll be here for the wedding."

Shelby bit her lip. She'd missed so much work already. But if she was home by Monday she'd still have plenty of time to get the Riley cake done. Kathryn would be able to handle anything that came up between now and then. "Of course." She warbled a smile.

"Goody." Same ol' Delilah.

Of course staying would mean another few days with Ritt, but once she got those papers signed it would be totally worth it.

"Are you still in California?"

"Yes."

Shelby barely had time to answer before Delilah shot another question her way. "You're not...?" She made a twirling motion between Shelby and Ritt.

"Oh, no. No." Shelby shook her head for emphasis. "So how have you been?"

"Great. There's the wedding and then I've been—you know what? There's entirely too much we need to catch up on. I'm calling Craig right now. The four of us need to get together for supper tonight. Won't that be fun?"

Shelby could think of plenty of things to call it, but fun wasn't among them.

"You don't have to do that—" Ritt protested, but Delilah had already connected to her fiancé. She plugged her ear with her finger and turned away as she spoke into the phone.

Ritt turned his blue-gold gaze to her.

Shelby did her best to smile and not cringe.

From the look on Ritt's face she wasn't successful. "We don't have to—"

"I don't like this any better than you do, but we both know we have to. They were our best friends," she said.

"Key word 'were.' That was a long time ago and some of us have moved on." Somehow his words sounded like an accusation.

Before Shelby could open her mouth to retaliate, Delilah turned around, a huge smile on her pretty face. "It's all set. We'll meet at Craig's tonight for dinner."

"Great." Ritt said the word, but Shelby knew he'd rather eat fire ants than spend any more time with her. Not that she cared. She felt the exact same way.

****

Craig's turned out to be an upscale condo perfect for an up-and-coming attorney with aspirations for City Hall.

Shelby locked the door of the rental, dismayed to see Ritt's rusty old Ford already in the lot as she made her way up the flower-lined walk. Two hours tops and she would escape and head back to…Ritt's house.

Staying in the same building with Ritt was proving to be harder than she had originally thought. Then again, when she imagined her plan, the final result—him signing the papers— happened after only one night of being under the same roof. Maybe even before. But her husband was proving to be a tougher nut to crack. Why he wouldn't sign the papers to begin with was a mystery in itself. Bitterness, she supposed, though she would have never thought Ritt one to cave to petty jealousies. And yet she couldn't say that she wouldn't feel the same in his shoes. He was exactly where she left him. Living in his parents' house, driving the same broken-down truck, working part-time at the bait shop. His time for baseball was over, he evidently hadn't gone back to further his education. He was stuck in a rut and blaming everyone else—her—for his lack of success.

Shelby raised her hand and knocked on the smooth black door.

Delilah answered within seconds as if she had been waiting on the other side for Shelby to show up.

"You made it." Delilah took a step back to allow Shelby to enter, then gave her a quick sisterly hug. "Come in, come in. Craig's putting the final touches on dinner. Would you like a glass of wine?"

"That'd be great. Thanks." As much as she tried not to look in his direction, her gaze automatically slid to Ritt where he lounged on the couch with a beer balanced on one jean-clad knee. Remarkably enough, he looked as at home on the expensive black leather sofa as he did the worn-smooth floral chintz that his mother had owned since Shelby had known them.

Ritt nodded in her direction, his gaze steady on hers. Shelby felt a shiver of familiarity run down her spine. Once she had a glass of wine, she peeled her gaze away from her husband and took a long, fortifying drink.

"Did you say Craig is cooking?"

Delilah nodded. "He loves to cook. It's like his Prozac, which is fine with me."

Craig came out of the kitchen, wearing an apron over slacks and a loosened tie, and wiping his hands on a dish towel. "Everyone ready for a salad?"

Ritt was instantly on his feet. Without even a glance at her, he made his way to the dining room. It seemed her husband was no more excited at having dinner with her than she was with him.

****

Craig was a surprisingly fine cook. Arugula salad with raspberry vinaigrette, veal parmesan, tender pasta, and sweet tiramisu for dessert. But as enjoyable as the meal was, Shelby couldn't get over the fact that she was once again seated across from her husband, his gaze focusing on everything but her.

Shelby took another long drink of the sweet red wine. Somehow she'd lost count of how many glasses she'd had. But was she honestly expected to remember something so trivial when faced with the roguishly handsome visage of her husband? "Let's take our coffee into the living room."

Ritt patted his stomach and to her dismay shook his head. "I should be getting home."

Perfect. Ritt could go home, and she could stay and visit. "I don't know about coffee, but I could use a refill." She held up her empty wine glass as evidence.

A look passed between Delilah and Craig.

"What?"

"You've had enough wine, Shelby." Ritt's words were quiet and kind. Exactly what she did not need from him.

"What are you now, my mother?" She instantly regretted her words.

"You didn't eat much," Delilah pointed out.

Okay, so she hadn't eaten that much, and she had downed her fair share of the wine...maybe a little more than. She felt warm and cozy, but she certainly wasn't drunk.

"Fine," she said, proud that her words were strong and true and not as blurry as her mind felt at that moment. "Coffee in the living room it is." What did it matter if she drank caffeine this late? With Ritt so close, she'd be up all night anyway.

She pushed herself up from the table, grabbing the edge as the room gave a quick lurch.

"Whoa." Craig reached out a steadying hand, and Shelby resisted the urge to swat it away.

"I'm fine." She smiled.

Delilah turned to Ritt.

He gave a grim nod.

"What?" Shelby asked.

Craig gave her a smile, the kind a person bestowed on drunks and children. "Ritt's going to drive you home."

"What? No. That is so not necessary."

"But it is," Delilah chimed in.

"Not." Shelby crossed her arms in front of her, hoping that she wasn't swaying as much as she felt she was. So she'd had too much to drink. She'd call a cab and...

Randall didn't have a cab company. She couldn't drive, that much she could accept, but that didn't mean she had to go home with Ritt. Maybe she could stay here.

She turned to Delilah intent on doing just that but realized before she asked how crazy the request would sound. She was staying at Ritt's house—a plan that should have resulted in him signing the divorce papers had he not been so stubborn—it was only natural that he be the one to take her home.

"Fine," she grumbled, wishing she could start the evening over again. Stupid hindsight.

She gathered her purse, and she and Ritt said their goodbyes to Delilah and Craig.

Ritt opened the passenger-side door, and Shelby slid inside.

The truck smelled as it always had, like old motor oil and Armor All.

Her heart beat with anticipation as he made his way to the other side and climbed in next to her. Back in the day she would have scooted across the bench seat to snuggle up under his right arm. The townspeople had joked that it had taken two to drive the old Ford. She and Ritt had laughed and gone about their business of being in love.

But that was a long time ago.

Without a word, Ritt cranked the engine, locked it in gear and turned the grill toward home.

Shelby kept her eyes straight ahead as they drove, concentrating on fighting off the memories that zoomed around inside her head.

She had never had a doubt back then. Ritt loved her and she loved him. That was all they needed to know. Everything else would fall into place. Ah, the arrogance of young love. Or was it innocence? She wasn't sure anymore.

Twenty minutes and not one word later, Ritt pulled up in front of the little white house.

Shelby opened the door before he killed the engine and was waiting on the porch when he slid from the cab. So much for distancing herself. She'd forgotten the key she had taken from under the mat and now she had to wait for Ritt to unlock the door.

She didn't move fast enough. He reached around her and shoved the key into the lock, giving it a vicious twist.

Why was he so angry?

She cut her gaze to his darkened features. His jaw was set, a little muscle jerking next to his ear. Without thinking, she lifted her hand and ran her fingers down the twitch. It was only natural from there to push her fingers into the hair at the side of his face and bring his mouth to hers.

His kiss was like coming home. His taste as familiar as her own. The shoulder strap on her handbag slipped, and her purse landed with a thump. She raised her other arm to slide it around his neck as his snaked around her waist and hauled her close.

His mouth ravaged hers. It had always been this way between them. Hot, volatile, borderline insane. That was how he made her feel, crazy with wanting him.

She was about to tell him so when he wrenched himself away. Shelby pressed the back of a hand to her mouth, wondering how things had gotten out of hand so quickly. It was unnerving. Thankfully, her relationship with him was over. She couldn't go through her life out of control.

"Ritt?" She didn't know what she was going to say, but it seemed something needed to be said.

"Go sleep it off, Shelby."

She was about to protest when he turned and stalked back to his truck. She didn't know how long he stayed gone, but he still wasn't home when she finally drifted off to sleep hours later.

****

Ritt stared at the back door of the house and twisted another cap off yet another beer. He pushed the hammock into motion and wondered if it was safe to go back in. How asinine was that? He couldn't go into his own house because his wife was inside. Slightly drunk, incredibly desirable. And driving him completely out of his mind.

If he had any brains left at all, he'd sign her blessed papers and send her packing, but some demon inside him couldn't let her off without a fight. He couldn't let her walk away a second time without paying a few dues.

That was all it was. He wanted her to sweat it out, wonder, pay the piper so to speak before she could have her freedom. He'd let her go, eventually. He had to, but that didn't mean he had to make it easy for her. No sir, he'd let her go all right, but this time when she walked away, she would know exactly what she was giving up.

Chapter Four

Bright morning sunlight cut through Shelby's sleep like a white-hot knife. She groaned and rolled over, pulling the pillow to cover her face and block out the brutal sun.

Two heartbeats later she remembered why her head hurt so bad and why her stomach pitched. She would like to blame all her problems on the wine she'd had the night before. More than half had to do with Ritt.

Why had she thought it a good idea to kiss him? Well, she hadn't really thought, she'd just done. Now she regretted throwing herself at his feet. It might not have hurt so much if he hadn't turned her down.

But even as the thought crossed her mind, she knew it was for the best.

With another groan, she rose from the bed. No time like now to face the music and find Ritt. She pulled on her Kmart robe and padded into the kitchen.

She was spared having to come up with a logical explanation for her amorous intent last night because Ritt was gone. In his place was a quickly scribbled note.

Gone fishing.

Naturally.

There was nothing more important right now than sitting on the lakeshore with a pole in the water. Certainly not signing divorce papers so she could get on with her life.

Shelby growled and crumpled the paper into a tight ball. She pitched it in the trash and grabbed a granola bar from the cookie jar.

She should have expected as much, she thought as she ate. Classic Ritt. Not one care about anything other than fishing and baseball. How did he support himself? Certainly not with a part-time job at the bait shop. He still lived with his parents for pity's sake!

And speaking of parents, she should call her mother right now. The earlier the better.

Maybe today Shelby could catch her before she left the house.

She dug her cell phone out of her purse. Dead, of course. "Grrr…" She'd have to go into town and get a new charger today. Damn Ritt's stubborn streak. It was costing her a fortune. She tossed her phone back into her purse with a frustrated sigh.

"What's wrong?"

At the sound of his voice, Shelby nearly jumped out of her skin. She pressed a hand to her heart and turned to face him. "Ritt! You scared me half to death."

He raised one dark brow. "Obviously."

"I thought you were fishing."

"It's nearly ten. They stop biting when the sun gets up."

If there was one thing she knew, it was that Ritt could stay at the lake all day without any problems. "You don't trust me in your house."

He shrugged. "Can you blame me?"

She supposed not. After all, she *had* set fire to his kitchen yesterday.

"Having a good morning?"

Why was he standing so close to her? She moved a step back and shrugged. "I was going to try calling Mom again."

"This is really bothering you, huh?"

Shelby tossed back her hair. "Naturally. You are accusing my mother of...of..." What exactly was he accusing Stormy of? "I'd like to call her and get this straightened out as soon as possible. Where's the phone?"

She tried to escape him again, those magnetic eyes and alluring...everything else.

The phone base was on the desk right inside the living room, but the receiver was not on it.

She looked around, moving a packet of papers and a newspaper clipping in her search.

Then Ritt was there, edging her away and finding the phone among the mess. Like there was something on the desk he didn't want her to see.

Phone in hand, she glanced down at the stacks of papers. Electric bill, junk mail, bank statements.

Ritt grasped her arm and pulled her back into the kitchen.

She glanced over her shoulder. "Why, Ritt...are you hiding something from me?"

For the merest moment he looked...guilty, then his expression reverted back to his usual devil-may-care. "My life is an open book."

"A very short book." Shelby immediately wished she could call back the snarky remark. What did it matter to her if Ritt wanted to waste his life lounging at the lake and working part-time at the bait shop? It was no skin from her schnozz if he had no ambition beyond the city limits of the tiny Texas town. He might not be the biggest go-getter around, but that was no reason to be mean.

He cocked his head to one side then released her. "You wound me, Shel. We're married. We're supposed to be on the same team."

"We wouldn't be married if someone would sign the papers."

Ritt shrugged then opened the refrigerator and studied the contents. "Of course, it would be easier if you would stop hiding stuff from me."

"I have nothing to hide."

"Oh yeah, Miss Finalist for a James Beard Award two years running?"

Shelby didn't know what to say. "How did you know about that?"

"I googled you." He emerged from the fridge with a bottle of water in hand.

"Google?"

Ritt nodded and unscrewed the cap. He took a drink then pointed the bottle mouth toward her. "You really should get out more."

"I should get out more?" She wasn't the one living…no, existing in Nowhere, Texas.

Ritt nodded, a smile twitching at the corners of his mouth.

Suddenly all she could think about was the night before, pressing her mouth to Ritt's, him kissing her back, at first reluctantly, then with the same passion they had shared so many years ago. Except it was different now, with a more controlled urgency. Or maybe that was the wine.

The heat that filled her left no room for argument. She shrugged it off. She wasn't about to get into another battle with him. He was pushing her buttons on purpose. For sport. This time she wouldn't be a part of his game. "You gonna call her?"

"Mom? Right. Of course." Calling her mother again wouldn't do any good. When Stormy Patterson didn't want to be found, it was useless to go looking. Still, it beat the hell out of reliving last night over and over in her head.

Shelby dialed the number and not surprisingly got her mother's voicemail. Even less of a surprise, it was full so she couldn't leave a message. With a sigh, she hung up.

"She not answer?"

Shelby shook her head. "You know Mom."

Ritt nodded in reply, and Shelby was proud of him for not commenting further. There had been no love lost between her mother and her husband.

The clock ticked off seconds between them. Shelby wondered if he was as caught up in yesteryear as much as she. She wanted to ask but was unable to form the words.

"Why did you come back here, Shel?"

The question was so quietly spoken that at first she thought she had imagined it. "It's time, don't you think?" She didn't add what it was time for—he knew.

Ritt shrugged but didn't meet her gaze. "I s'pose." Then he grabbed his shirttail and pulled the garment over his head.

Anything else she had thought to say vanished in an instant. She could only stare at the mouthwatering planes and rippling muscles of his chest. As if last night's kiss hadn't been enough.

Her husband seemed oblivious to her drooling as he wiped his forehead on the shirt.

He wadded it in one hand and propped his fist on his hip.

"What?" he asked innocently as she continued to stare.

"I…I mean…" Before she could form a coherent thought, the shrill ring of the phone cut between them.

Shelby's heart gave a painful thump. Ritt's gaze locked with hers as he answered.

"Hello? Slow down, Delilah. Okay." He handed her the phone. "It's for you."

She pressed the receiver to her ear. "Hello?"

"Oh my gawd, Shelby! I'm so glad I caught you. I need a cake."

"What?" Her brain was still a little fuzzy from the wine, and it had nothing whatsoever to do with Ritt's little striptease or his thigh brushing against hers as he reached into the cabinet above her head. It was almost as if he was trying to distract her.

"The baker called. She fell waterskiing this weekend and broke her wrist. She's in a cast up past her elbow and won't be able to work for at least four weeks. I need a cake!"

"For the wedding?"

"Of course, for the wedding. Can you do it?"

Ritt picked that moment to move away. Shelby gulped in a big breath of Ritt-free air, clearing her head of his intoxicating presence.

"I would love to, Dee, but I don't have any of my stuff here and—"

"I'll buy whatever you need." Desperation dominated her tone.

"I don't have an oven big enough or a freezer."

"We can use the fellowship hall at the church. Isaac won't care."

"Isaac?"

"You remember Isaac Yancy. He's the pastor there now."

Shelby didn't have time to contemplate the fact that the wildest boy in their class was now the leader of the biggest church in town.

"I'll pay you double," Delilah continued, "and buy all the ingredients. Please, Shel. I don't know what I'll do without your help."

Of course she couldn't leave her friend in the lurch. "I can't promise you anything elaborate."

"Anything is fine." Delilah's voice lost its desperate edge. Shelby heard her heave a big sigh of relief. "Thanks, Shel. You're the best."

****

Shelby spent the rest of the afternoon in Amarillo gathering supplies. Cake pans, flour, eggs, milk, sugar and so forth. Her plan was simple, make a test cake of her favorite recipes and have Delilah and Craig decide which one they liked the best.

Once the recipe was firm, she'd move the operation to the church kitchen and start baking and freezing.

Luckily, the guest list for the wedding was smaller than she would have thought. Cake for two hundred was a snap compared to the six or seven hundred that she had first envisioned.

Ritt was nowhere to be found when she pulled her rental into his driveway that afternoon. Lord only knew where he was. Fishing...drinking...both.

He seemed to have no ambitions, loafing about with no direction. She refused to believe that she was responsible. He had made his own choices, and she hers. She had opted to get on with her life, start a bakery, and make something of herself while Ritt...hadn't. So he'd given up his baseball scholarship. They had all made sacrifices. Yet she didn't understand why he seemed to not care about anything these days.

She hauled the last of the bags into the house and started putting away the perishables. The fridge was almost empty, home to a container of ketchup and a few bottles of beer.

By the time she finished unpacking the dry goods, she heard the crunch of gravel from the driveway. Ritt was home.

She was plugging her cell phone into the brand-new charger when he sauntered into the kitchen.

How a man could make a ratty T-shirt and even rattier jeans look so yummy was mindboggling. Shelby swallowed hard and went back to her task.

"You get everything you needed from town?"

She nodded, avoiding his gaze. "I'll bake tomorrow."

"Good, then come on."

She looked up and met his steady gaze. "Where are we going?"

"To the movies."

"I don't think—"

"Come on, Shelby. There's nothing to read into this. It's mindless entertainment. Now let's go."

How could she fight that kind of logic? Okay, so the truth was she didn't want to tell him no. "All right," she said as if the idea wasn't thrilling. While inside her heart gave a lurch of joy.

The drive into Amarillo was short and familiar. Sitting beside him as if there wasn't anything between them. She turned her attention to the road in front of them, though her gaze kept straying to her husband. So much was the same, the way he pushed his hair back from his face only to have it fall over his eyes once again. The way he tapped his thumbs against the steering wheel in time to whatever was playing on the radio. And so much was different. The barbed-wire tattoo that seemed to move of its own accord as his biceps flexed and relaxed. The braided leather bracelet he wore around one wrist.

Ritt pulled into the parking lot and killed the engine. "What?" he asked.

Had he known that she was staring at him, that she couldn't take her eyes off him for more than a second?

"What are we going to see?" Shelby asked as she slid from the truck.

Ritt shrugged. "Whatever's showing. They play classics every Friday night so there's always something good."

The next movie was about to begin. Ritt bought two tickets while Shelby loaded up on snacks at the concession counter.

But her heart sank as the movie started. It was a chick flick, the story of a woman so desperate to have a baby she hired her male BFF to be the father. Any other time Shelby might have enjoyed the movie, found it whimsical and entertaining, but sitting next to Ritt... More than one time before the credits rolled she had to wipe tears from her eyes. She hoped against hope that he didn't see her cry.

The sun was setting when they exited the theater. Shelby stopped, her hand on the door handle of the old Ford while she watched the sun splash orange, pink and purple across the endless Texas sky. She had missed the wild sunsets during her time in sunny California. Everyone there thought the sun setting on the ocean was the most beautiful, but they had never seen the endless sky in Texas.

With a sigh, she climbed into the truck and tried her best not to think too much about the movie. Instead she focused on the cake she was about to decorate for her friends. But that made her think about the wedding scene in the movie and the chubby baby. Then the baby she lost and the man sitting beside her.

She chanced a quick peek in his direction. His expression was unreadable, both hands on the wheel, gaze locked in the forward position. His shoulders were relaxed, but it was too casual to be anything but a front to hide what was going on in his own mind. What good would it do to bring it up now? It was water under the bridge as they say, and she had burned that bridge a long time ago.

****

They rode in silence all the way back to Randall. Ritt drove through town and without a word pulled into the driveway.

Shelby picked up her purse and opened the door. "Thanks for the movie."

"Yeah." The one word was all he could manage through the knot of remorse in his throat.

He waited a heartbeat before following her into the house.

She was in the kitchen, staring into the refrigerator.

"Hungry?"

She shook her head. "I ate too much popcorn."

"Me too."

She flipped on the light and made her way into the living room. He followed behind her, somehow needing to remain connected to her. "Do you ever wonder...?" He shook his head.

"Wonder what?" She gave him a questioning look, not realizing the turmoil raging within him.

"What would have happened if...he would be in school this year, huh?" He swallowed hard against the lump in his throat.

She gave him a wistful smile. "First grade."

He imagined himself taking a dark-haired tyke to school, Spiderman backpack on his shoulder and a Transformer smuggled in his pocket. He pushed the image away. It hurt too much.

"I blamed myself for years." Her quiet words fell on his ears.

"It wasn't your fault."

"I know that here." She pointed to her head. "But it's hard to convince here." She covered her heart with her hand.

Tears welled in her eyes.

"Don't cry." He eased down next to her on the sofa, wrapped his arms around her and pushed her head to rest on his shoulder.

They stayed that way for countless long minutes as they soaked both strength and remorse from each other. Ritt blinked back his own tears and continued to hold his wife. Hold her the way that he should have held her so long ago. But back then, full of pain and misery, she had pushed him away figuratively and literally as she tried to deal on her own.

Maybe her coming back was a good thing. Maybe now they could heal some of these past hurts. Maybe...

"I'm okay." She pulled away from him, sending another jagged crack through his heart.

He stood and pushed his hands into his pockets to keep from reaching for her again. Pulling her close and never letting her go.

"Everything happens for a reason, right?" She wiped the tears from her cheeks with the back of one hand.

He didn't answer, couldn't find the reason why they lost the baby, unless it was to get Shelby out of Texas. If she had never left, then she wouldn't have started her bakery.

She wouldn't be getting the respectability and acclaim that she deserved.

"I think I'll take a shower."

He nodded, still not trusting his voice. He should let her make her escape, allow the moment to pass. No sense dwelling in the past and things that could never be.

****

The sun had truly set as Shelby finally made her way out of the bathroom. She performed every grooming ritual she could think of in order to waste as much time as possible. Being held in Ritt's arms was almost more than she could bear. But she had kept herself together out of self-preservation alone. Only Ritt held the power to break her heart with a look, a whisper and a touch.

She had come back to Texas for one reason and one reason only: to divorce him. Allowing

73

herself to linger in his arms was not part of that plan.

She pulled the peach-colored T-shirt over her head and slipped into the gray pair of yoga pants she had picked up along with all the baking supplies. Hopefully she had sequestered herself long enough that Ritt had gone to bed. There would be no sneaking into his room, into his bed to tease him. Truth was, her little charade was a sweet torture to her as well. Nope, that plan had definitely backfired. She grabbed her clothes from the bathroom floor and tiptoed down the hall. The flicker of the television met her before she turned the corner back into the living room.

Ritt slouched on the sofa, bare feet propped on the coffee table, a beer in one hand. Shelby stopped in her tracks, the sight of him taking her breath away. It was too domestic, too familiar, him lounging on the couch, T-shirt riding up to reveal a tantalizing peek of rock-hard abs. Clyde's chin propped on one denim-clad thigh.

That teenaged girl hidden inside her wanted to nudge the dog aside and curl up next to her husband. If only there was some way to turn back time, go back to when everything was right between them, those early spring months before graduation, before it all fell to pieces.

"I'm done in the bathroom."

He gave a quick nod then raised the beer bottle to his lips, never once taking his eyes from ESPN.

She couldn't stop her feet. They carried her to the couch. Then her traitorous knees bent and before she knew what she had done, she was sitting a hair's breadth from him. If he noticed, he didn't say anything, just continued to watch the scores as they rolled across the bottom. Braves, Royals, Rangers, Cardinals. He should have played for one of those, maybe even be playing for them still.

"Why didn't you play baseball after I left?"

He stopped, beer halfway to his lips, then shrugged. "That time was over, Shel."

She shook her head. "How could that be? Baseball was everything to you."

Something she didn't recognize flashed through his dark eyes, then as quickly as it came, it was gone. "I had to give up my scholarship."

"You could have been a free agent."

"Not in August. The professional season was winding down."

"But what about the next year? You could have gone pro then, right?"

"A year without playing? No one would pick me up then." His voice had turned flat, hiding whatever he was feeling inside. Regret swamped around her. She had left, gone away to California so he could get the life he deserved. But it didn't happen that way. What good had her leaving done? None, none at all. She had lost him and the baby, he had lost her and baseball. So much pain tucked away, hidden from view, but now brought to the surface.

She wanted to lean into him, press a quick kiss to the corner of his mouth, the way she used to do when they found themselves like this, her bored and needing him, him watching scores and getting his "man time" on.

But those times she had done that, gave him that little kiss, entwined her fingers into the hair at the nape of his neck, his attention on the TV had quickly shifted and she found herself flat on her back, underneath his warm weight, all pretense of interest in baseball scores flying away on the West Texas wind.

She scooched down the couch and laid her head on the throw pillow farthest away from him. The sound was turned all the way down on the television and the voiceless men on the screen chatted and smiled as they flashed highlight reels and injury reports.

"Are you ready to go to bed?"

His innocent words sent a heat searing through her.

She adjusted the pillow and settled a little deeper into the couch cushions lest she crawl right into his lap.

"No, I'm fine."

He cleared his throat. "I mean, I can go in the other room if this is bothering you."

"Nuh-uh." She pushed her feet down, unable to stop them as they went in search of his heat. It was a timeless position for them. In those early days of their marriage, she'd be worn out from the pregnancy, needing more rest than usual, feet cold despite the Texas summer heat.

You have to stop thinking about him, about all those sweet days.

She jumped when she felt his warm touch on her arch. Before she knew what happened he had pulled her feet into his lap, lightly massaging each toe, the curve of her arch, the hills and valleys of her ankle.

The touch was familiar and ancient, part of another time, another Shelby, another Ritt.

They let themselves into the house quietly, stifling giggles with kisses. It was three in the afternoon. Miracle of miracles he didn't have baseball practice. His mom would still be at the bank, his father at the plant, and with any luck, Kyle would be at the library. They'd have the whole house to themselves.

It wasn't often that they had this sort of luxury. Usually they were stealing kisses behind the dugout.

"Kyle?" Ritt smacked her hand away as she ran it up under the bottom of his Randall High Cougars T-shirt. "Stop that." He growled, but his laugh and quick kiss took the sting out of his words. "Kyle?" A little louder.

"All clear?" she asked, sneaking her fingers under the hem of his shirt once again.

She couldn't help herself. She loved to touch him, warm skin, taut muscles.

"All clear." He swung her up and closer to him.

In one smooth move, she wrapped her legs around him and buried her face in the warm sweet curve of his neck.

She inhaled in anticipation. She loved the way he smelled, like laundry soap and leather.

"Shelby?" The sound of her name on his lips brought her back to the present, back to her very real husband and his very real touch. Except now his fingers had slid under the leg of her yoga pants and had stilled against her skin.

His other hand reached out and he laced fingers with hers, gently tugging her up and closer. Before she could breathe either a protest or an encouragement, he leaned in and pressed his lips to hers.

Past and present merged into one as he kissed her. Slowly at first, little nips and touches, then deeper until her head began to spin from the wonder of it all.

The feel of his lips on hers was as natural as breathing. Why had she been fighting this? What was the point when being held in his arms felt so good…so right? And it was so much easier to melt into his embrace and not worry so much.

She wrapped her arms around him, sighing as he lifted his mouth from hers. Then his warmth was gone and she found herself sitting on the couch alone.

"Ritt?"

He shook his head. "Goodnight, Shelby."

She watched him go, doing her best to pull herself together. She had fallen prey to her own game, to the close proximity to the one man who knew how to get to her better than anyone else.

A bitter laugh escaped her. She had almost lost sight of what was important, almost let the past get the most of her. But there was only now, her wanting a divorce. Him, not willing to give it to her. And she'd do well to remember it.

Chapter Five

Ritt let himself into his house the following afternoon, the smell of sweet cake wafting about him. It was a welcoming smell, almost as alluring as the soft floral scent his wife preferred these days.

He shook his head. Last night, them, the movie; it was almost too much. It had taken everything he had to kiss her then walk away, but he had to have her wanting him, wanting to be with him, wanting to make everything between them work once again.

That was the plan. Yep, he finally admitted it to himself. He wanted his wife back. Probably always had.

And she wanted him, at least physically. He could see the light of desire in her eyes, hear the quickening of her breath whenever he touched her, but he wanted more. He wanted her love.

Craziest. Thing. Ever.

"Shelby?" he called.

"In here."

He made his way into the kitchen, expecting to find a chaos similar to the night she'd made them dinner. Instead, everything was neat and orderly. Cakes stacked and looking delicious.

"And you didn't even use a cake mix?"

"Bite your tongue."

Ritt watched as she spread the last of the creamy frosting onto the third cake. She was about to pitch the butter knife into the sink full of soapy water when he plucked it from her fingers.

"You can't waste perfectly good icing that way." He licked the icing from the flat edge, surveying the cakes scattered across his mother's sideboard. "This is fantastic."

She smiled her thanks. "If I always licked the spoon, I'd be as big as a house."

"You never had to worry about your weight before," he said, wondering if she had already submerged the icing bowl into the sink full of soapy water. She shrugged. "Things change." Didn't he know it.

"Craig and Delilah should be here any minute." As she said the words, the couple turned into the driveway.

Shelby untied the apron from around her waist and pulled it over her head.

He was still reeling from the fact that she couldn't cook a simple casserole but she could bake a scrumptious-looking cake. But the real test was still to come.

"Shelby." Delilah beelined for her friend, wrapping her in a tight hug. "I can't thank you enough for doing this for me."

"I'm happy to."

Delilah released her and nodded toward Ritt. "I meant what I said about paying you double."

"No way." Shelby shook her head. "This is my gift to you."

Tears welled in Delilah's eyes.

Ritt looked to Craig.

He shrugged.

Women.

"Hey," Shelby said, pulling Delilah in for a hug.

Delilah swiped at her tears. "I'm sorry. This has been so stressful. One thing after another. The bridesmaids' dresses were the wrong color and the tux place lost all the measurements, now the cake."

"But it's all corrected now, right?" Shelby asked.

Delilah sniffed with a nod.

"Then there's nothing to cry about."

"Amen," Craig mouthed.

Ritt had the feeling that his friends had been fighting. If he had to guess, it was over something stupid about the wedding. See? Weddings were

82

nothing but trouble. The two people most likely to survive the statistics were arguing over paper napkins and ribbon color.

Delilah gave her a watery smile. "You're right, of course. Level-headed Shelby."

Ritt rolled his eyes. Level-headed Shelby who cut him off at the knees every chance she got. Who wouldn't talk about the problems between them. Who wanted to divorce him and leave him in the dust once again.

"Now, come try the cakes."

She cut the three of them a piece of each cake. "These are my best sellers: raspberry filled, lemon zest, and Italian cream."

Ritt took a big bite of the first piece and resisted the urge to groan out loud. It melted the moment it hit his tongue, beyond delicious, a little slice of heaven in his mouth.

"You made this?" Craig asked, his mouth stuffed full of cake.

Shelby nodded. "Now I know it's all the rage, but I don't like to work with fondant. It doesn't have the same taste as frosting. But if that's what you want…"

Delilah shook her head and took another bite of the cake. "I want what's here."

"I'll add icing flowers and embellishments, maybe some ribbon and fresh flowers to match your colors."

83

Ritt was surprised at how professional she sounded. He shouldn't have been. Shelby had made good for herself. He should be proud, not amazed.

"Which one is your favorite?"

"All," Craig said emphatically. "We want one of each."

Delilah nodded. "And we'll pay triple."

"Would you stop with that? I'm not charging you a dime."

"Did you try this one?" Craig lifted a forkful of the raspberry-filled to Delilah's lips.

Their eyes locked as she obligingly ate the cake off his fork.

Ritt shifted, suddenly uncomfortable with the intimate moment.

"Delicious," Delilah murmured. She licked her lips as Craig watched her, his gaze never leaving her mouth.

"I'm sorry," Craig said.

"Me too." She pulled his mouth to hers and kissed him like there was no tomorrow.

Ritt ran a hand across the back of his neck. Shelby looked everywhere but at the happy couple. He wondered if other people had felt the same way when he and Shelby had been so close. He felt like a peeping Tom in his own house.

He cleared his throat.

After what seemed like half an hour, but truly could have only been a few seconds, Craig lifted his head. "No more arguing. The wedding is going to happen whether the dresses are midnight or sapphire."

"Yes," she murmured.

"So." Shelby rubbed her hands together. "I'll start the cakes tomorrow morning. And they'll be ready for your wedding Saturday afternoon."

Craig and Delilah nodded.

"I'll need access to the church and the name of the florist who's doing the flowers."

"The church has already been arranged. You'll have access to the kitchen both Friday and Saturday morning. Here's the card for the florist."

"Thanks, Shel," Craig said, bussing her cheek. "You're the best."

"I don't know what we would have done without you," Delilah added.

Ritt was beginning to wonder that himself.

****

Shelby hand dried the last of her new pans, all the while decorating the wedding cake in her head. She needed to get her ideas down on paper before she lost the details of the design. The time restraints alone would necessitate a more simple design, but more often than not, simple was synonymous with elegant.

85

She heard a thump, a clank, and a muffled curse. Ritt.

He'd disappeared right after Delilah and Craig had left, and Shelby knew he was avoiding her.

She sighed. It was for the best. After that kiss... One of them had to keep their wits about them.

So Ritt had gone out to work on his truck while she planned a wedding cake and wondered when she'd be able to leave. Now she knew she was stuck in Texas until Saturday evening, but considering that Ritt was the best man, she knew he'd be involved in all sorts of wedding activities that would take his attention away from finally signing the divorce papers.

Her stomach pitched. It was what she wanted, she told herself. To be free.

From outside, Ritt's truck started. Shelby peeked out the kitchen window, hoping he wasn't leaving. The hood was up and his long, denim-clad legs the only part of him she could see.

She tried not to sigh in relief that he was staying. The whole idea was ridiculous.

She found a pen and paper and started sketching the cake. There would need to be a focal point, one cake taller than the other two. That way each flavor would stand alone.

The shrill ring of the telephone cut through her thoughts. She set the notebook aside and went to the phone base, but the receiver wasn't there.

She'd let the machine get it. She sat back down and started drawing once again.

The phone continued to ring, then the answering machine picked up. Seconds later her mother's voice filled the kitchen.

"Hey, baby girl. Sorry I've been incommunicado, but you know…"

Shelby jumped from the stool and raced around the kitchen, looking for the phone. "Got your message and well, we'll talk when I get back." Get back? Where was she going?

Shelby lifted the stacks of newspapers on the kitchen table, checked under the pile of bath towels in one chair to no avail. She raced to the living room. "I'm going to be hard to reach for a couple of days."

"Mom! Mom!" Like she could hear her.

"Me and Mickey are going island camping overnight—have you met Mickey?"

"Don't hang up," Shelby yelled to no one.

"He's a k-e-e-p-e-r."

Shelby growled and started digging through the couch cushions.

"Oh, gotta go." Her mother's voice sounded distant, as if she had taken her mouth away from the receiver.

"Don't hang up!"

"They're ringing the bell for last boarding. We'll talk when I get back. Ciao, baby girl."

A-ha! She found the phone under a fishing magazine on the coffee table. She hit talk. The phone clicked, and the line went dead.

With shaking hands she punched in the number. The phone rang and rang, but no one picked up. Only her mother could disappear in the blink of an eye.

Shelby collapsed onto the sofa in defeat.

The screen door slammed, and Ritt called out, "Shel, you okay? I heard shouting."

He hadn't even bothered to wipe the grease from his hands. A trickle of sweat ran down the side of his face, starting under the band of his baseball hat and dropping off the edge of his firm jaw.

Shelby groaned again. "Mom called."

"What'd she say?" He took off his cap and wiped his face on the bottom of his T-shirt.

Shelby tried not to stare at the rock-hard abs hidden underneath that lucky cotton. But her mouth went dry despite her best efforts. How she wanted to go over there and run her hands up under that thin fabric and feel the warmth of him.

"Shelby? What'd she say?"

"Huh? Oh." She dragged herself out of the fantasy world and into reality. "I couldn't find the phone."

His long legs ate up the distance to the answering machine. He punched the playback button and listened to her mom's message.

"There you go," he said, a triumphant smile on his face.

"What are you talking about? She said she'd call back in a couple of days."

"If she was innocent, then she wouldn't need to call back. She would have denied it, and that would have been that."

Shelby shook her head. "This is my mother we're talking about."

"True, but I still think she would have defended her innocence, even if she promised to call back."

Most likely he was right, but there was no way in hell Shelby was giving up that easily. "Whatever." Not the most brilliant comeback, but the best she could do under the circumstances. He was standing too close to her. And he smelled so good.

"You just can't believe that she would do anything wrong, can you?"

"I didn't say that." She sniffed. Her mother had done plenty wrong, but most of it boiled down to her hippie-bohemian-new age

89

philosophy. Shelby didn't even know who her father was. She was certain her mother knew but wasn't telling. With her luck he was some aging rock star with more children than sense.

That was the exact reason why she needed this divorce. She wanted respectability and honor. She deserved it. She had worked damned hard building her business. It was time to move on.

Shelby pushed herself up from the sofa. "I'm going into town to get the ingredients for the cakes."

Ritt shook his head, his expression telling her without words that he thought she was running away from their conversation. Like she cared what he thought.

"Whatever," he grumbled.

"Right." She grabbed the keys to the rental and headed out the door.

****

Two hours later she pulled into the drive, thankful to be done. Well, she still had to bake the cakes tomorrow. An exhausting prospect, but well worth the joy of her friends.

She was barely out of the car when Ritt came out to help her take the groceries inside.

Bag after bag, they hauled her purchases into the house. "Damn. All this for one cake?"

She shrugged. "They wanted all three flavors, then I've got icing to make and the groom's cake. I figured chocolate cupcakes. You think that'll be okay?"

Ritt nodded. "Chocolate was always Craig's favorite."

"Yours too."

"Yep."

She was all too aware of his steady gaze on her as she loaded the perishables into the fridge and stacked the other supplies on the counter.

Once the chore was complete, she propped her hands on her hips and surveyed the kitchen. "Now for dinner."

He shook his head. "No way. You're not cooking in my kitchen again."

"I baked cakes in it yesterday."

"Totally different." He took her by the elbow and steered her toward the door. "Let's head over to the diner."

Walking into the diner was like stepping back in time. Others thought so too. All eyes were on them as they made their way across the small eatery.

"Land sakes alive." Fannie George greeted them as they scooted into a booth. Fannie was as much a part of Ned's Diner as the chili cheese fries. "I never thought I would see this day."

"Hi, Fannie."

"Shelby McCoy, what brings you to town?"

Shelby opened her mouth to correct her, but closed it instead. She was Shelby McCoy, for a little while longer anyway.

Ritt adjusted his hat and sat back in his seat. Was he waiting to see what she would say?

Strange, but it seemed almost as if Ritt wanted to stay married to her. Could it be that what Craig said was true? That Ritt felt she hadn't given them a chance after she lost the baby?

Nah, that couldn't be. He was toying with her, kissing her, then leaving her all alone on the couch. He was tying her in knots, and he knew it.

"I'm here for...the wedding." She couldn't very well tell Fannie she had come to get a divorce from Ritt. The whole town assumed that had been taken care of a long time ago.

"Ain't that somethin'? Delilah and Craig finally getting hitched and you and Ritt back together. Love is a wondrous thing." Fannie winked like she held the secrets of the world in that one simple statement.

"We're not—" she started with a shake of her head.

"Fannie, I'm parched. Can you bring me an iced tea?" Ritt smiled at the woman with all the charm of a movie star.

"Of course, sugar. Shelby, you want a tea?"

"Unsweetened, please."

Suddenly she felt put on the spot. No one drank unsweetened tea in this diner. "Calories, you know," she mumbled by way of an explanation.

Fannie threw back her head and laughed. "You almost had me goin' there. I'll be right back with y'all's drinks." She stuck her pencil back behind her ear and sashayed to the counter.

"You don't have to try so hard to prove that you don't belong here anymore."

Shelby blinked, hurt by his words. "Is that what you think I'm doing?"

"What is it then?"

"Do you know how many tablespoons of sugar are in one glass of that tea?"

"Why can't you relax and enjoy yourself? You used to."

But that was a long time ago, when she had to accept her plight in life, daughter of a hippie mother and an unknown father. Shelby had only lived in Randall for two years, having moved around time and time again as her mother looked for whatever was missing from her life.

Well, she had a great life now. She was no longer searching. She had found her niche, baking and decorating cakes. And she was good at it. She had clients lining up for her confections. With her business growing she had only one choice: get her divorce from Ritt before he realized he could have half of what she had worked so hard to build.

Shelby sniffed. "I don't know what you're talking about."

Ritt studied her with those all-knowing eyes. One look and he stripped away her every layer of protection and delved beneath to the scared little girl she had buried inside.

"Here ya go." Fannie slid their drinks in front of them and waited patiently for them to order, not realizing the moment she had interrupted.

They ordered their usual. Even after all this time, Shelby remembered how Ritt liked his cheeseburger and the fact that he preferred mustard to ketchup on his fries.

She pushed all thoughts of calories from her mind and drank three classes of tea as they ate. Not because Ritt was right and she needed to relax, but to show him that she could.

It was well past eight when they pulled into his drive.

Neither one spoke as they entered the house. A sweet sadness swept through Shelby. How many times had they come home like this? But back then if they'd had the house all to themselves, they would have made out like crazy on the living room sofa, with the hurry of getting caught and the urgency of youth.

She sneaked a peek at Ritt from under her lashes. His jaw was a bunch of twisted muscles. Was he thinking the same thing? How wonderful it was back then. How awesome and perfect.

"It would have never worked, you know." Her words surprised her. She hadn't meant to say them.

"We'll never know now." He stalked away, skulking into the living room and turning on the TV.

"Ritt, I—" So many things came into her mind all at once, but only one truly needed saying. "I'm sorry."

He kept his gaze fixed on the baseball game as if his very existence depended on it. "Me too, Shelby. Me too."

****

Ritt kept his eyes forward until he was sure she was gone.

Damn it but if he had any sense in his head, he would sign the papers before she drove him completely insane. But he didn't have any sense. Hadn't had any where she was concerned for a long time.

Having her this close but still out of reach was killing him. He should have kicked her out on her fanny that first night and saved them both a lot of trouble.

The phone rang, and he reached over to answer it, not bothering to check the caller ID. If he had any luck in the world, it would be her mother calling back to admit she had taken his parent's bribe. But his luck didn't seem to be holding out today.

"Ritt?"

"Hi, Mom." Just what he needed.

"Hey, sweetie. Your dad and I wanted to call and check on you."

Ritt smiled. Like most mothers, his had a sixth sense when it came to her children. She always knew when something was bothering him or his kid brother, Kyle. "I'm fine."

"Tell me again and maybe this time I'll believe you."

Ritt took a deep breath. "Shelby's here."

A second beat between them before his mother answered. "Oh, Ritt."

He swallowed hard, feeling like he was nineteen again and his heart was breaking anew. "She wants a divorce."

"We're coming home." His mother's voice was stern with love and determination.

"No. Don't. I'm fine."

"You don't sound fine."

He didn't, but if he kept pretending he was, that Shelby wasn't rubbing salt in old wounds, then maybe eventually it'd be the truth. "I just need some time."

"Are you going to give it to her?"

"I don't think I have much choice." He didn't bother to tell his mom that Shelby had sent the papers long ago and he'd been putting this moment off for months. Or that he had been desperately trying to devise a way to win her back.

"Wayne, turn around. We need to go home."

Ritt sat up straight, planting his booted feet on the hard planks of the floor. "No. Seriously, Mom. She'll be gone before you get here."

"You need us, and we're coming home."

Ritt shook his head at her resolve. He did need his family right now, but he could always drive to Lubbock and spend the week with Kyle. "I'm fine," he said.

"We'll be home in a couple of days," she said despite his protests. "Maybe by Sunday afternoon."

"Sunday night." He heard his father yell.

Ritt smiled. "You don't have to, you know."

"Yeah, sweetie, we do."

He knew his mom would answer that way. "Be careful."

"We will. And Ritt...we love you very much."

"I know. I love you too." He hung up the phone and turned to Shelby who stood in the doorway from the hall. How long she'd been there he wasn't sure.

"I take it that wasn't my mom."

Ritt grabbed his beer and sat back. He adopted his I-don't-give-a-shit attitude and flashed her a cocky smile. "Nope. It was my mom."

Shelby shook her head. "Why do you do that?"

He took a drink of his beer to soothe his suddenly dry throat. "Do what?"

"Get all…" she waved a hand in front of her, clearly at a loss for words. "Get all cocky and arrogant."

"I don't know what you're talking about."

She slammed her hands onto her hips. "You do."

"Not." He hated how juvenile he sounded, but he couldn't let her know his secret.

That it was the only defense he had against her.

"Whatever." At least she sounded as childish as he did. "I'm going to bed." It was barely nine o'clock, but he didn't point that out.

He stood and stretched. "Fine by me," he said, starting for the door.

"Where are you going?"

He stopped two steps shy of his goal. "Wow, Shelby. You sound suspiciously like a wife." Then he slammed through the door and out into the night.

****

It was after three when she heard him, his careful footsteps shuffling through the kitchen. Something rattled, as if he'd bumped into the curio cabinet where his mom displayed her collection of blown-glass figurines.

Clyde barked.

Ritt hushed him.

She heard another small crash and rose from the bed.

He was drunk, and she'd better go help him before he destroyed his mother's house.

"Shelby." He opened his arms wide as he caught sight of her. His grin stretched from ear to ear and if she hadn't known better, she'd have thought he was actually glad she was there.

But she had heard the solemn tone when he had talked to his mother. Her presence was taking its toll on him. Did he think he was the only one hurting? A myriad of emotions swamped her. Being back in Randall brought up more memories than she cared to relive. Some good, some not so good. And others…well, they were heartbreaking.

"Come here and give me a kiss."

Shelby crossed her arms in front of her and planted her feet. She hoped the stance looked secure and firm when in reality it was to keep her from taking him up on his offer.

"You and I both know that's a bad idea."

His baseball hat was pulled down low, the bill shadowing his eyes. "There was a time when we thought it was a good idea."

Memories of those times were the ones that haunted her the most. "That time is over." Hopefully he was too far gone to hear the crack in her voice.

Being here, being so close to him was getting to her. If she hadn't promised Craig and Delilah that she'd make their wedding cake, she would leave right now. Throw a shirt over her nightgown and head straight for the airport and out of his life.

Ritt braced an arm against the wall, balancing himself as he tried to pull off his boots. He wobbled, and Shelby was there in an instant, supporting him in his efforts.

"We weren't so bad together. Right, Shel?"

"I don't think now is the time to talk about that, Ritt."

"Can I tell you something?" He continued without waiting for her answer. "I've missed you."

Shelby swallowed back the knot of regret that formed in her throat. "I don't think it's the time to talk about that either."

He gave a jerky nod and started toward her. His feet were suddenly steady. Maybe he wasn't as drunk as she had originally thought. By the time she realized his intent, it was too late.

One arm snaked out, wrapping around her and pulling her to him. His lips captured hers, swift and sure. Her knees buckled with surprise and desire, but he was there to hold her up. And she was lost.

Her fingers went to the bill of his hat, tipping it up and off his head like she had done a thousand times before.

Memories teemed around her, fueled by the night and his lips on hers. All the days she had spent in his arms, in his bed. Regret mingled, but she pushed it away. She should do the same to him, push him away. Fight the passion rising to the surface.

But she had been fighting her feelings for so long she didn't have the strength anymore. Or maybe it was the desire. It took so much to protect herself. So much to pretend that this wasn't what she wanted. That he wasn't what she needed.

She sighed, melting into him. And he pulled her closer still, turning and walking her toward the bedroom.

She forced herself to pull away. "Ritt, I—"

"We were good together, Shel." He kept moving.

She kept letting him. "That was a long time ago."

"This feels like now."

And now felt amazing...wonderful...right.

He pulled his shirt over his head, and her heart pounded in her throat.

Who was to know but the two of them?

She didn't protest as he nudged open the door to his room and urged her inside. Didn't protest when he stripped her T-shirt over her head and lowered her to the bed.

A sigh escaped her lips as he moved away, trailing kisses down her neck, across her collarbone, into the hollow of her throat.

"I've dreamt of this, you know. Holding you again." One callused hand moved from her hip to the curve of her waist and higher still to palm her waiting breast.

His touch was filled with warmth and comfort, all the things she had been missing in her life.

Suddenly respectability wasn't so important anymore. Not if she could have this, this fire blazing between them. This love burning her from the inside out.

He had changed little in the years they had been apart. His chest was a little broader. She traced her fingers across the star-shaped scar just under his collarbone. "What happened?"

He chuckled, low and sexy. "Fishing accident. Took a lure for the team." She leaned in and kissed it.

He stopped laughing, sucking in a sharp breath as her tongue met his bare skin.

"Shelby," he groaned.

She raised her head. "What?" Her gaze met his. She wanted him to see the light in her eyes, the desire and longing she held only for him.

"Nothing." He dipped his head and kissed her again.

Shelby fisted her hands in his hair, holding him to her, perhaps even trying to hold on to him forever.

Then he pulled away. His hair slipped between her hungry fingers, her body chilled as he moved his heat from on top of her.

"Where are you going?" she asked, still reeling. Her head was spinning with desire, her heart full to bursting with the realization that she loved him. She had always loved him. Her Texas husband.

"Condom," he said, digging through the nightstand drawer. "Can't have a repeat of last time."

Shelby's heart fell into her toes. She felt as if a bucket of snow had been dumped on her desire.

Ritt froze, realizing he'd said the wrong thing. His eyes reflected the regret that turned down the corners of his mouth.

"Shelby." He licked his lips as if they had suddenly gone dry. "I—"

"Don't." She held up a hand as she reached for her clothes. Her insides were raw with the realization that she loved him, but he didn't love her back. How could he, if he said things like that to her?

Humiliation snaked through her. Degradation, remorse. She shouldn't feel that way. She and Ritt had shared equal responsibility in making the baby that changed both of their lives. But she had been the one who wasn't able to carry the child, nurture it and make it grow.

She grabbed her shirt and pulled it over her head, not bothering to turn it right side out. Or around. The tag tickled under her chin as she shook her head. "Don't, Ritt."

He ran his fingers though his hair, massaging away whatever demons plagued him.

Shelby scrambled to her feet, using his moment of weakness to be strong. He opened his mouth to protest or lie to her once again, but she ducked her head and hurried from the room. Down the hall she fled, him right behind her.

"Shel?" His vice was soft and questioning as she stepped into his parents' room. She shut the door between them before he could follow.

"Good night, Ritt." She was proud of how steady her voice sounded, even though her knees trembled and her hands shook as she turned the lock.

"Shel? Shelby!"

She crawled back into the bed, surrounded by his scent and memories, and somehow managed to hold the tears at bay.

****

Ritt stared at the old wooden door that separated him from the only woman he'd ever loved.

"Well, you've really done it this time, McCoy," he muttered to himself.

He gave the door one last look, then turned back to the kitchen. He stopped momentarily to pick up his hat, slapping it against his thigh before settling it back on his head.

He needed a cold shower to wash away the heat of his desire and the last vestiges of alcohol clogging up his system.

But it was late…or early, depending on how he looked at it, and he was tired.

He made his way back into his bedroom, wondering how one man could be so stupid.

Without bothering to change clothes, he flopped onto the bed. Pulling the pillow over his head in a poor attempt to stop the parade of memories behind his closed lids.

He hadn't intended his caress to be more than a simple, sweet kiss. He just wanted to touch his lips to hers and then sleep it off. But he should have known that nothing was simple where Shelby was concerned.

In the span of one heartbeat, he'd sobered up and fallen prey to an even bigger intoxicator—his wife.

It was a short ride to hell from there. Or was it heaven?

He had no defenses where she was concerned, no way to block out what she did to him, his love for her. All-consuming, ever-burning, more than he could even understand.

A wet nose nudge his hand, then Clyde whined and gave him a reassuring lick. A second later, the mattress dipped with the canine's solid weight.

Ritt expelled a heavy breath. He hadn't meant to hurt her. Once the words were out, he wanted to call them back. The hurt in her eyes was like a physical blow to his heart.

Any chance he had for winning her back had been blown away with that one sentence. A stupid thing to say to the one person he loved more than the air he breathed.

Ritt had spent more than one night half-drunk, with only the canine for company and dreaming of Shelby. Why should tonight be any different?

He scratched the dog behind one floppy ear and drifted off, dreaming of being her one and only once again.

Chapter Six

Sunlight cut like a knife through hot butter, slicing into the best dream he'd had in a long time.

Ritt flopped onto his back, flinging an arm over his eyes to block out the cruel light.

He wanted to sink back into the bliss of the dream, but his head was pounding.

And through the pain came a familiar heartache.

He rolled over, burying his face in the pillow. He breathed in deep. Shelby.

Last night came crashing back. He and Shelby at the diner. His parents calling. Tying one on at the Longbranch, coming home, and... Shelby.

With a groan, Ritt wiped the last of the sleep from his eyes and rolled from the bed. He owed her an apology. An explanation. Something. She wouldn't forgive him. And he couldn't blame her.

Just more bloody water under the bridge.

He stumbled through the house, stopped in the bathroom to splash water on his face and tried to get a handle on the day.

He made it to the kitchen. There was no note from his wife, and the coffee was cold in the pot. She must have left a long time ago. Then he remembered. It was Friday. She was baking cakes for Craig and Delilah. Tonight was the rehearsal dinner.

Ritt poured himself a cup and stuck it in the microwave. As it nuked, he peeked outside. Both his truck and Shelby's rental were missing from the driveway. At least he'd had enough sense to get a cab home.

That must have cost a pretty penny. The Longbranch was halfway to Amarillo. But it was amazing where Ben Franklin could get a man when he had the notion. He'd been safe last night and that was good, but now he'd have to get a ride back to the honky tonk to reclaim his old Ford. With a shake of his head, he picked up the phone and called Craig.

****

"I can't believe you're working today." Ritt shot Craig a pointed look.

"Well, not everyone can call in sick on a whim."

"Jealous much?"

Craig returned his look. "No."

Funny thing was, Ritt knew he meant it. Craig was on top of the world. He had a thriving law practice, and he was about to marry the girl who was meant for him and take her on a honeymoon to paradise.

The thought of his own honeymoon flitted through Ritt's mind. If one could call a weekend in San Antonio a honeymoon. Maybe if he'd taken Shelby someplace special. Like he could have afforded that back then. He'd been nineteen, dependent on his parents for damned near everything in his life. Maybe if they'd used that five thousand dollars to make Shelby stay instead of entice her mother to leave…

He shoved the thought aside. He'd forgiven his parents a long time ago, and he truly couldn't find fault with Stormy Patterson for taking their money to start over. None of it, not even one iota, was Shelby's fault.

"You okay, buddy?"

Ritt nodded. "Right as rain."

Craig turned into the parking lot at the Longbranch, pulling his Mercedes alongside the beat-up Ford. "You know, people lie to me for a living."

"Yep," Ritt said, his hand on the door.

"When you want to talk about it, you know where I am."

Ritt opened the door, stepping out into the graveled lot.

"Maybe if you told her the truth," Craig said, leaning over to look at Ritt.

"Then she'd stay for all the wrong reasons."

"I meant the truth about how you feel about her."

Ritt shook his head. "See ya tonight." He slammed the car door and crunched his way to his truck.

****

Shelby blew her hair out of her face and promised herself that she would give Kathryn a raise when she returned to LA. Making a wedding cake without her faithful assistant's help showed Shelby how much Kat really did.

It had taken the better part of the day, but she had completed the three triple-layer cakes and the multitude of chocolate cupcakes in lieu of the traditional groom's cake. Tomorrow she would ice the cupcakes, add the fresh flowers and use the matching ribbon to tie the wedding cakes together. All in all, they would be beautiful in their simplicity.

She wiped down the counters one last time, then grabbed her purse and shut the door to the fellowship hall.

All evening long she'd heard the commotion from the rehearsal going on in the sanctuary, and she wished to be a part of it. But being in the kitchen while people that she had known since she was in high school were laughing and having a great time, just proved the distance between them. She didn't belong here. She was a Cali girl now. With any luck, she'd have her signed papers by tomorrow afternoon and would be on her way back home.

The thought should have made her happy, but a sigh escaped her as she unlocked the rental car and started back to Ritt's house.

He'd probably still be out with the wedding party, eating and whooping it up for the last time.

She hadn't talked to him all day, but that didn't mean he hadn't crossed her mind. Crossed was a bad term. She baked cakes for a living. She could do it in her sleep. Even with three cakes on her to-do list, memories of Ritt had sauntered in and hijacked her thoughts for the day. Not long-ago memories, but new ones. More potent than the ones from years before.

Last night, almost making love with him. She had to keep reminding herself that he'd been drunk. But that didn't erase the scent of him from her mind. He should have smelled like a brewery, but he hadn't. He'd smelled like...Ritt, and that alone was enough to make her forget all the things she had promised herself.

And then he said the worst possible thing to her and the memories came crashing back. Not the good ones, but the ones that seared her straight through.

Ritt's truck was in the driveway when she pulled in. She didn't worry about parking behind him; she'd be up and out the door long before he even stirred in the morning.

She let herself into the house, surprised to see the flicker of the television as she set her purse on the kitchen table.

"Home already?"

Ritt nodded. "Since it's a day wedding, Delilah wanted everyone to get a good night's sleep. Dark circles and pictures." He shrugged. "You know Delilah."

Shelby nodded, the air suddenly thick.

"I'm sorry about last night." His words were soft, but carried the weight of the world.

A small laugh escaped her. But it was sad really how much the sound resembled a sob. Shelby pressed a hand to her mouth and gathered her composure. Now was the time to start. Now was the time to harden her heart to all things Ritt. "Sorry that you kissed me or sorry that you said..." She waved a hand around, unable to repeat his words from the night before.

"Sorry that I hurt you."

113

She wanted to scoff, tell him in a flippant tone that he didn't hold such a power over her, that mere words could wound. But they'd both know it was a lie.

Ritt patted the couch next to him. "Quit hovering and come sit down. You look dead on your feet."

Shelby hesitated, unsure whether to forge a ceasefire or protect her heart. But his expression was tired, his mouth pulled down at the corners. Could it be that he truly was sorry for the hurtful words that put a stop to what could have been the second-biggest mistake of her life?

She took a couple of hesitant steps, then sank down into the armchair across from him. It was the first time she'd been off her feet since the early morning. She'd eaten lunch standing up while a cake baked. They needed constant attention since she was working with a regular oven, and she didn't have time to make any mistakes. Her knees popped, and her stomach growled. She'd skipped dinner altogether.

Ritt rose from the couch and made his way to the kitchen, coming back in a few minutes with a plate full of chicken and pasta and a can of Coke. "I can't have the neighbors thinking I'm starving you."

Shelby smiled with gratitude and accepted the plate. Mentally she pushed away the thoughts of how long this fragile truce could last between them. "Where'd you get this?"

"Leftovers from the rehearsal dinner."

"Yummy." She polished off the food in no time, sitting with Ritt and watching some late-night show on television. She had a feeling he'd turned off the game for her. But she couldn't dwell on that. Him catering to her tastes seemed too intimate by far.

Suddenly the room seemed smaller and warmer. She snatched up her plate and took it to the kitchen, needing space from him once again. Perhaps they couldn't have this, a civil separation, a relationship squashed in the middle between red-hot lovers at each other's throats.

Needing something to do to keep her away from him, she washed the plate. And then the rest of the dishes in the sink.

"You don't have to do that, you know. The cleaning lady comes tomorrow."

Shelby jumped at the sound of his voice. She whirled around to find him right behind her. Close. Too close.

"You have a cleaning lady?" She had to say something to break the current that sparked between them. Was she the only one who felt this pull whenever they were together? The draw of him, the urge to lean in and taste the edge of his jaw, the curve of those masculine lips. With no thought to the consequences, the pain of tomorrow, the mistakes of the past.

He shrugged. "She comes a couple of times a week."

"Are you kidding me?" Her voice rose, her desire for him quickly turning to anger. "You work at the bait shop. Part-time. How can you afford a cleaning lady?"

His eyes narrowed until she couldn't read them. "What is it about the situation that bothers you, Shel?"

What indeed? And then she knew. "I have worked so hard in my life to find happiness. I struggle every day. You just float along, satisfied with whatever life hands you. It's not fair, damn it."

He stared at her for a full three seconds then took a half a step closer, forcing her up against the cabinet. "You think I like how my life turned out?"

"Y-yes." Unable to find room for her hands between them, she braced them against his chest. A big mistake she realized as her fingers encountered his heat. "My life's all right." His eyes were hooded. "But there's one thing missing."

"What?" she whispered, her heart thumping painfully against her ribs.

"This." His mouth crashed down on hers, and Shelby's world tilted on its axis.

Her hands traveled up his torso and linked behind his neck, silently begging not to end the passionate onslaught. His arms snaked around her, hauling her against him and telling her without words that he wasn't going anywhere.

Then his lips left hers. She was about to protest when he angled his head the other way and began to kiss her again.

She should stop him, but all of her senses were so tuned into him that she couldn't raise even a single protest.

His hands slipped under the edge of her T-shirt, easing around to cup her hips in his palms. He used his hold on her to show her how much he wanted her, how far gone he was himself, before he lifted her and sat her on the kitchen counter.

He snuggled into the vee between her knees, kissing her still. His mouth reluctantly left hers as he broke contact to pull her shirt over her head.

Shelby sucked in a gulp of air. Fortified herself for the next dip of his head. The kiss was intoxicating, heady and powerful.

She followed his lead and yanked his shirt over his head, loving the feel of those rock-hard muscles beneath her fingers. Once their kiss had been broken, he stared into her eyes, his gaze

117

giving away nothing but the passion that burned between them.

Shelby basked in the sensation of his hands on her, as rough and callused as they had been so long ago.

He slid his arms around her again, his nimble fingers deftly unhooking the straps of her bra. Ritt took a step back, breaking their kiss. Her breasts spilled out of the beige lace.

Eyes closed, she heard his sigh a second before she felt his mouth on her.

Ecstasy.

She wrapped her legs around his middle, securing him to her. Ritt grunted his approval, slipping his hands underneath her fanny and lifting her off the cabinet.

Nothing else concerned her as he carried her through the house and into the bedroom.

He laid her crossways on the bed, unbuttoning her jeans, and stepping back to pull the denim from her legs. She watched him from underneath her lashes, her eyes almost closed in anticipation.

He didn't break their only contact as he stripped off his own jeans and briefs, standing before her proud, naked and aroused.

He seemed to be taking his time as he moved in for another kiss. This one just as electric. Even though he touched her nowhere but lips to lips, it was no less powerful. She wanted to scream for him to hurry, beg him to slow down, swear he'd never let her leave.

She wrapped her arms around him, pulling him to her. And then he was there, on top of her, warm, solid, hard. Hands re-exploring valleys and curves that they'd conquered long ago.

Shelby sighed as he smoothed one hand over her hip and lower still. She bit back his name, afraid that the sound of her voice would somehow break the spell that surrounded them.

His kiss was magic, transporting her to another world. His lips trailed down the valley between her breasts, his tongue tracing a pattern of nothings all across her stomach and lower still.

She could only thread her fingers through his hair and hold onto him as he carried her to heights she had only dreamed about since she'd left Texas.

He nipped his way back to her parted lips, kissed her again, then shifted their weight. She lay sprawled across his chest, loving the feel of him under her as much as the feeling of being under him. Maybe it was being close to him that made it so good. Close and naked.

Her fingers had been missing him all these years, but the muscles under her palms belonged to a man that she had only glimpsed. Every little ripple more than it had been. Every ridge more than before.

She slid her hand between his thighs and traced the length of him. He flinched in response, a quick chuckle escaping him. She remembered and explored. All the familiar that was her husband. All the new that was the man he had become.

She kissed those new ridges, the scar on his shoulder, the little birthmark on his hip.

He threaded his fingers through her hair, fisting his hand in the long tresses and urging her mouth back to his and once again using his strength to reverse their positions.

But instead of his warmth, she felt the cool brush of air as he readied himself. He slipped into a condom and was back in an instant, capturing her lips in a scorching kiss.

He wedged his knee between her thighs, urging them apart so he could settle between them. His weight was her only anchor to the earth, his warmth holding her to him as he pressed for entrance.

Then he was there, filling her, loving her. She met him stroke for stroke, finding the rhythm they had discovered so many years ago. Their lovemaking was the same and yet different, familiar yet new.

The man knew what the boy hadn't forgotten. Where to kiss for maximum effect, how sensitive her neck was to his touch, how to drive her crazy with his hands and mouth.

She wanted to scream his name to the heavens as the pressure built inside, but somehow she kept her silence, afraid that if she made a noise the dream would be shattered.

The only sound was their breathing, the urgent pant of desire.

She wrapped her legs around him as he quickened the pace, carried her to heights she barely remembered existed. But they were real, and the only way to get there was in his arms.

He slid one hand under her and lifted her to him as he thrust one last time. She shattered into a million pieces as he strained and stilled, reaching his own pinnacle.

This was not what she had come to Texas for. Nowhere in her plans had she thought about sleeping with her husband. Rekindling the passion that sizzled between them.

Her heart beat wildly in her chest, her limbs trembling. She was still wrapped around him but her hold had gone slack. He was still inside her, hard but still as he struggled to regain control. His heavy breath stirred the strands of her hair. His face buried in the curve of her neck.

She couldn't see his face, didn't know how he felt. Couldn't fathom what they were to do now.

"Yo, bro?" The moment was lost as a greeting called out from the entryway.

Ritt groaned, but this one was different from the last. He shifted his weight, flopping onto the bed beside her.

Shelby rolled away, snatching up the robe she'd thrown across the chair that very morning.

"Ritt? Mom and Dad said I should come check up on you—holy cow. I know you're here, there's a bra on the kitchen floor. I'll just get my stuff from the uh, car..." The creak of the wheelchair floated in through the open bedroom door. They hadn't expected any company.

"Shel, I—"

Shelby shook her head. "Go see about Kyle," she said, then started for the bathroom, fighting back tears with every step.

She shut the door behind her, the robe hanging inside swaying with the motion. Shelby pressed herself against the wood, leaned her head back and closed her eyes against the tears.

How stupid could one girl be? She took a deep shuddering breath and pushed herself toward the sink.

Her arms were stiff and robotic as she went through the motions: turn on the water, pull back her hair. But the face in the mirror was a shocker. Her eyes looked smoky and heavy-lidded, her lips puffy and pink. Her neck and chest splotchy with the force of his kiss and the rasp of his beard stubble against her skin.

She shuddered with the memory. Funny how mere thoughts of him turned her on. No, not funny. Pathetic. It was pathetic that she was putty in his capable hands. Willing to fall into bed with him like nothing bad had ever happened between them. Like the last seven years hadn't mattered at all.

She splashed water on her face, wet a washrag and pressed against the red marks marring her skin. There was one in particular that would most likely bruise. Just what she needed. She was damned-near twenty-six years old...she was a successful business owner, and tomorrow morning she would wake up with a hickey. Simply fabulous.

"You're supposed to put toothpaste on it," Delilah said. *"And then press it with a spoon."*

"I tried that. It didn't work."

"Here. Let me." Delilah stepped toward her, pulling her collar down. "Damn, girl. What did y'all do?"

Shelby winced, and gingerly touched the love mark Ritt had left on her collarbone.

123

"Just be glad you don't have a father. My dad would kill me if I came home with that."

Shelby ignored the father comment. Delilah was always saying something like that, and Shelby turned a deaf ear where it was concerned. "Do you think my shirt's enough to cover it?"

Delilah laughed. "If it's a turtleneck it will."

Shelby smacked her on the arm. "Be serious. It's a hundred and five in the shade. I can't wear a turtleneck."

"Uh-huh. Maybe you should have thought about that before." Delilah shot her a smirk and handed her the tube of Crest. "I'll go get a spoon."

Shelby shook away the memory, pressing the cool cloth to the circles below her eyes as she tried to ignore the voices from the other side of the door.

Kyle must have gotten his things from his car. Now the brothers were catching up. Talking baseball scores and fishing holes. Shelby wanted to crawl into a hole of her own and stay there until after the wedding tomorrow.

At the rate she was going, she'd never get Ritt to sign the papers. After the last half hour in his arms, she wasn't sure if she even wanted them signed. But one thing was certain, she had to get out of Texas before he broke her heart in two.

124

She sucked in a deep breath and took her hair down, running her fingers through the strands. Then she let herself out of the bathroom and crept back into the bedroom. It was too early to call it a night, and it wasn't like Kyle wouldn't know she was there eventually. The only thing to do was face this problem head on.

Her bra was lying on the bed, obviously put there by Ritt. She willed back the heat that filled her face and concentrated on getting dressed. She pulled her yoga pants back on and slipped her T-shirt over her head. These were the only clothes she had that wouldn't look ridiculous for her to have on at nine o'clock at night.

But she knew the mark on the side of her neck was shining bright for all to see. The only solution would be to pull on one of Ritt's button-downs. Like that would look less intimate.

Shelby shook her head and started for the living room.

Play it cool, she told herself.

She stepped into the entryway and gave a rainbow wave. "Hi, Kyle." So much for playing it cool.

"Shelby." Kyle's boyish face split into a grin as big as the West Texas sky. "Come over here and see me."

She tucked a wayward strand of hair behind her ear and resisted the urge to chew on her lip as she crossed the living room.

"How have you been?" She leaned down and gave him a peck on the cheek.

He nodded. "Good," he said, but his voice sounded a bit distracted. Then his eyes widened as he put two and two together and came up with what had been going on before he had interrupted.

Of course it didn't help that Ritt's hair was standing on end, his Levis unbuttoned at the waist and his T-shirt was on wrong side out.

"Ritt didn't tell me that you were here."

"Oh." She looked over to her husband, not sure what she expected to see. He raised his beer bottle in salute and shot her a grimacing smile.

"I came back for—"

Behind Kyle, his brother started shaking his head.

"I came back for—"

"The wedding. She came back for the wedding," Ritt interjected.

"Oh." Kyle nodded.

"I came back for the wedding," Shelby said with a quick nod.

"Yeah…" Kyle said slowly.

"Ritt, can I talk to you please?"

"Right." Ritt pushed himself to his feet and hurried to her side. It was obvious that he was no more comfortable facing off with his brother than she was. "Be right back, Kyle."

They walked into the kitchen, the elephant in the living room following close behind.

She turned to face her husband and took another step back when she realized how close he was to her. Close enough that if she leaned in a little she could trace the line of his throat with her finger. Or her tongue. She closed her eyes and took another step back.

"Ritt," she said, opening her eyes and staring him full in the face. Now was not the time to be timid where her husband was concerned.

"Why didn't you tell him why I'm really here?"

"Does it matter?"

It did, but she couldn't tell him why. Every time he told someone his version of the truth it made her wonder if perhaps he didn't want the divorce. Was that why he wouldn't sign the papers?

She let out a pent-up breath then waved a hand as if to clear the words between them. "Do whatever you want." She started to push past him, but he hooked her arm and pulled her against him.

How perfectly she fit to him from every angle. Her back was pressed against his front, his warm breath stirring her hair and sending goose pimples cascading down her arms.

"Do whatever I want? Is that an invitation?"

She shook her head while she searched for her voice. "You and I both know what happened tonight was a mistake."

"Uh-huh…" He lifted her hair off the nape of her neck and pressed a whisper of a kiss against the sensitive skin there.

She couldn't stop her shudder, or her sigh. Instead she closed her eyes and prayed for strength. "A mistake," she said stepping away from him. "One that cannot be repeated." Shelby pushed herself out of his arms and out of the kitchen. This time Ritt let her go. He'd proved his point. One kiss and he could make her squirm. Make her wet and ready. But it had the same effect on him.

He grabbed a fresh beer, adjusted the crotch of his Levis and eased his way back into the living room.

Only his brother remained.

"Where's Shelby?"

Kyle shrugged. "She said she was going into the other room to watch television."

Ritt flopped back onto the sofa and eyed his baby brother. "You didn't have to come home, you know."

"I had laundry to do anyway," Kyle said with a shrug. "At least now I know why Mom called. How long has she been here?"

"Six days."

"Six days?"

Ritt nodded.

"Six days? She's gone for six years and in less than a week you've already talked her back into your bed."

"She's been gone seven years." Seven years, two months, and twelve hours. But who was counting?

"You know what I mean."

Ritt took a swing of his beer and shook his head. "It's not like that."

Kyle raised a brow, his smirk saying it all. "Then what's it like?"

"She wants a divorce."

"Not if she's sleeping with you."

"It's not like that," Ritt said again, sucking down his beer and wishing for something stronger. Like that would help. One touch from Shelby was so intoxicating to his senses even moonshine paled in comparison. "For as long as I've known her, Shelby has wanted to be stable and respectable. Now she's got a shot at everything she's always wanted. I can't blow that for her." He hadn't realized until he said the words how true they were.

129

Guilt swamped him. He had been manipulating her from the start, not signing, teasing her, kissing her, when all she wanted was a fresh start.

"And you aren't respectable?"

"I work at the bait shop. I live with my parents. I'm still driving the first truck I ever bought."

Kyle snorted in disgust. "Why do you do this?" He shook his head. "Why do you sell yourself short? Drive yourself down?"

Ritt stood on suddenly wobbly knees. He held his arms up as if to embrace the room. "This is it," he said, gesturing to the room at large. "This is my life. This is who I am. I can't change for anybody. I don't want to change."

"Not even for Shelby?"

"You don't get it, do you? I'm so seven years ago."

"Oh, I get it all right. You're afraid to show her who you really are, because if you do and she rejects you then, what do you have? At least this way you have a chance." All the anger drained out of his voice. He shook his head. "I never thought I'd say this, but I feel sorry for you, Ritt."

"Don't bother." He scoffed at the idea, but the words cut him to the core. Was he so easy to read, so transparent that his kid brother could see right through every excuse he had? "I'll go make your bed."

If he took that chance and it fell through, then he would be left with nothing. Nothing at all.

Chapter Seven

After avoiding Ritt for the rest of the evening, how ironic was it that he filled her thoughts so completely?

Kyle had gone to his room, and Ritt had slammed out the screen door that led to the back. That left Shelby alone in the bedroom, flipping back and forth, trying to get comfortable and trying to forget the sizzle of Ritt's lips on her skin.

She turned over once again, biting back a growl of frustration. She was pretty sure that Kyle was already fast asleep, but she didn't want to disturb him just in case.

Clyde gave a small woof and jumped down from the bed, his solid weight hitting the floor with a thunk. He scratched at the door, then turned to gaze at her with his sad eyes.

Shelby pushed back the covers and padded over to the pooch. "You wanna go outside?" She followed him out of the bedroom. He looked back every few feet to make sure she still followed.

He made his way to the back door, tags jingling and toenails clicking against the wood floor. He stopped at the screen door and sat back on his haunches. He whined, raised one paw and threw back his head as if to bay out his frustrations.

"I hear ya, boy." He whined again, and Shelby opened the door, watching the short-legged dog waddle down the steps.

Clyde trotted over to the dark form slung between two large trees and raised his head to give a little bark.

The sound of Ritt's voice floated over to her, his words unintelligible as he rubbed the dog behind the ears. Then he lifted the pooch into the hammock with him.

As if of their own accord, her feet carried her down the stairs and across the patchy yard. It wasn't the easiest thing to keep grass growing in the West Texas heat. It seemed as if Wayne McCoy had long ago given up the effort. Her bare toes encountered dry dirt and shoots of Bermuda as she walked toward Ritt.

"Nice night." Shelby gazed up at the sky, a billion stars twinkling from between the branches of the trees.

"Yep."

She sank to a thick ring of grass, no doubt the legacy of watering the trees. She pushed her toes into the dirt under the hammock, a patch most likely worn through from many feet pushing the hammock on nights exactly like this.

"Be still," Ritt whispered. "Just be still."

But how could she when he was buried inside of her, hard and throbbing? She wanted so badly to move with him, against him.

"Ritt."

"Shhh..." He pressed a kiss into her hair. "Let the motion take you."

Shelby swallowed down a moan and tried to relax. "What if someone comes out here?"

She hated the thought, but at the same time it made her want him more, this risk of being caught spurring her desire to greater heights. Ritt rocked against her, and she bit her lip to keep from screaming out his name.

He chuckled, seemingly pleased with himself for being able to push her to the edge of reason while remaining in control of his own.

"Ritt, please..."

He thrust one last time, covering her mouth with his, taking in her strangled cry of pleasure.

Ritt cleared his throat.

Was he thinking about that same warm spring night so long ago?

"You should be sleeping," he said.

"So should you."

"I can get by on a little."

Shelby smiled into the dark night. "Don't let Delilah hear you say that."

Neither one spoke, the night filled with other sounds. Nocturnal birds, cicadas and the occasional car from across town.

"Was it so bad here, Shel?"

She wrapped her arms around her legs and propped her chin on her knees. "It wasn't bad at all."

"And that's why you took off as fast as you could?"

"That's not how it went."

"Tell me," he commanded, his voice soft, his face hidden in shadows.

"I really believed that you would be able to get your scholarship back."

He answered her with a grunt.

"I knew that's what your parents wanted for you." She could barely make out the bob of his head.

"They're not as…committed as they were back then."

Shelby let out a small laugh. "Committed. That's a nice way of putting it."

The ropes creaked as he shifted to face her, suddenly his expression was clear, remorse and need filled his eyes. "They weren't as…"

135

"Committed," she supplied.

He nodded. "Committed until after Kyle's accident."

"So…what? They wanted you to live your life as well as his?"

"He was a kid, you know? One day he was running through fields and breaking windows with baseballs and the next he was half-dead. When they knew that we weren't going to lose him completely, they changed. They understood how precious life is. How it needs to really be lived."

"And they agree with how you live your life now?" She hated the derisive note in her voice. "That's not what I meant to say."

"There's nothing wrong with my life, Shelby."

She waited a heartbeat before responding. "Are you happy, Ritt?"

"Mostly."

"I guess that's what really matters."

"What about you, Shel? Are you happy?"

"Of course." But there was a too-chipper squeak to her voice that added a note of falseness to her words. "I mean, what's not to be happy about? I have a great apartment close to the ocean, I have a thriving business. I'm my own boss, and I love what I do."

"Is that all?"

"W-what?"

He cleared his throat. "Can you tell me one thing? And the truth this time. Why did you leave?"

She sighed into the night. Not wanting to answer, but needing to say the words all the same. "I wanted you to come after me."

The one sentence could have been whispered and still it would have rung through the night.

"You wanted me to come after you?"

She rocked back, needing some motion to balance all of the emotions lingering from the night. "I know it sounds silly, but I loved you so much. I was feeling a bit bruised after everything. I felt like I couldn't do anything right." She wiped the tears forming in her eyes. "I couldn't do the one thing every woman should be able to. I couldn't carry a baby. Your baby." She took a deep breath. "I felt like I let you down."

"Oh, Shel." His words were heartfelt and filled with more emotion than she could name. "You didn't."

"Then why?" She didn't have to add the rest. Why did she lose the baby? Why did they have to suffer? Why did their love get interrupted?

"I don't know."

"So this was supposed to happen?"

"I don't know that either."

"I thought if I left, and you got your scholarship back, then everything would be okay. But then there was this part of me that also wanted you to come after me. Maybe thump your chest a couple of times, tell the world I was yours, and then we'd live happily ever after."

He didn't say anything. Once again the night was filled with bobwhites and crickets.

"When does this pain stop?"

She shook her head. "I don't think it ever does."

"Then what are we supposed to do?"

She smiled quietly into the night. "All we can do now is learn to live with it."

Chapter Eight

Ritt ran a finger under the collar of the pristine white dress shirt and wondered how much longer he had to remain in the monkey suit. A while for sure, seeing as the wedding hadn't even started.

Craig looked remarkably calm for what was to be the biggest day of his life. He talked to his younger brother who was also dressed for the occasion, full tuxedo, white pleated dress shirt, sapphire-blue tie. Er, midnight blue.

Ritt pulled on his sleeves and tried to breathe normally, though he was certain the tie was slowly strangling him to death.

From inside the church sanctuary he could hear the murmur of voices, the buzz of anticipation as the guests waited for the wedding to begin. So much hype and pomp and ceremony for what could be accomplished in the justice of the peace's office in less than ten minutes.

"You ready?" Craig slapped one hand on Ritt's shoulder, startling him out of his thoughts.

"Wha...yeah," he said. "I'm ready."

139

As the organist played Pachelbel's Canon, the men filed down the aisle and took their places at the front of the church to await the bridal party.

Ritt resisted the urge to tug on his sleeves again, adjust his suspenders, loosen his tie. None of that would make the time go by faster. Or change anything...

"Your hands are like ice." Ritt rubbed Shelby's fingers between his palms.

"I'm scared," she admitted.

Ritt couldn't stop his smile. "What's there to be afraid of?"

"I don't know. Everything."

"You've got it all wrong," he said, still holding her hands in his own, lending her his strength. "This is the perfect beginning, don't you see?"

"See what?" Her gray eyes were enormous.

"Us...me, you and the baby."

"In your parents' garage—"

"It's detached."

"We can only stay there until the fall. Then what are we going to do?"

Ritt shrugged. "We'll cross that bridge when we get there."

She was stiff with tension as he pulled her to him. He lowered his head and kissed her sweet

*lips. Slowly, her form melted into his. And he
knew everything was going to be just fine.*

The organist played the first few bars of
"The Wedding March." The guests stood. Craig's
face lit up as Delilah turned the corner and started
down the aisle toward them.

Ritt shifted his attention. There was no sense
living in the past. He and Shelby, they'd had their
chance. They were no longer crossing bridges,
they'd all been burned.

And last night...?

He'd held heaven in his arms once more.

But it was morning now. And he had to stop
hanging on. Last night, their talk. It was good to
clear the air a little. Even if she didn't believe that
his parents had paid her mother to take her away.
Seven years had passed. What difference did it
make now? The deed was done.

"Ritt?" Craig's voice was a whisper of
urgency. "I need the ring."

"Oh," he said. "Oh." He reached into his
pocket and pulled out the little velvet box.

Inside was a three-carat diamond, perfect in
every way.

What would have happened if he had done
that for Shelby? Bought her a diamond, let her
walk down the aisle in front of all of her family
and friends, instead of hustling her to the

141

courthouse and repeating vows after a court official.

What was he thinking? Three days ago he'd been criticizing the masses for falling into the drivel that made up weddings. Now he was wishing that he had done more for Shelby.

A church wedding couldn't have changed what happened to them. There were too many other factors in place. His parents and their drive to make him everything that he could be along with all of the potential that Kyle had lost. Her mother and her bohemian ways. Shelby's hurt. His pride. And the baby.

"You may now kiss your bride."

Craig lifted Delilah's veil, and the congregation held its breath as he leaned in.

A few more minutes and Ritt would see Shelby again. His heart jumped at the thought.

Then reality set in.

They'd had a chance, and now it was gone. She was trying to start again, and he was standing in the way.

"You coming?" Craig's brother nudged Ritt's arm and pointed to the door that led to the fellowship hall where the reception was to be held.

"Yeah. Right." He followed the wedding party through the double doors, automatically looking for Shelby.

Part of him craved seeing her while the other part breathed a sigh of relief that there was no sign of her.

Only her cakes. They were spectacular, beautiful and elegant. He had to tamp down the surge of pride that had a smile quivering on his lips.

But seeing her talent was just another nail in the coffin that housed their marriage.

Regardless of last night, regardless of the love that he still held for her, he knew what he had to do.

****

Shelby propped her hands on her hips and took one last critical look at the cakes. They were beautiful, even if she said so herself. Given the circumstances, she was double proud of herself.

She sighed and rubbed her eyes. Today definitely felt like the morning after. She had managed to dry her tears and leave the bathroom long enough to say a quick good morning to Ritt's brother Kyle. He'd grown up while she was away.

Kyle had always been a kind and gentle soul. He wore his heart on his sleeve, unlike his brother whose every emotion was guarded as if it were gold. But Ritt hadn't always been that way.

Shelby shook her head. Once she'd said her greeting, she begged off any more visiting, citing a headache as she hurried to the church to give the final touches to the cakes.

Heartache was more like it.

She should be used to it by now. That was what Ritt was to her, a perpetual heartache.

Shelby added a couple of more lilies to the top of the middle cake. She tossed the stems in the trash as her phone rang. She snatched it from her purse, needing the distraction to keep her from bursting into tears once again.

"Shelby?"

"Mom?" She barely recognized her voice through the crackle and static.

"Sorry. Reception is really bad here, but I promised I would call."

"It's all right." Shelby took a deep breath to steady her nerves and muster up courage. "Mom, did Ritt's parents pay you to take me away from Texas?"

Her mother waited so long to answer Shelby thought the connection had been broken. "It's not that simple."

Her knees went weak. Shelby sank to the kitchen stool, glad the cakes were complete. Her hands were shaking so badly she wouldn't have been able to hold a decorator's tube if her life depended on it.

"Shelby?"

"I'm here," she whispered.

"I…it was a long time ago, and you were so emotional."

"Why didn't you tell me?" She swallowed hard against the lump in her throat. Ritt had been right. He'd been right all along. No wonder he had treated her with such contempt.

"There just never seemed to be a good time."

"I suppose not."

"Honey, don't blame Ritt. He had nothing to do with it."

"I know." Water under the bridge as they say. "It doesn't matter." But it did. Much more than it should have.

She had fallen in love with her husband all over again. No, that wasn't true, she had never stopped loving him in the first place. But there were too many bad times, too much heartache to give it a second chance.

Static filled the line. At first Shelby thought the call had dropped, then her mother's voice broke through the crackle. "Shelby, I—"

One of the ushers motioned from the doorway, the signal that people would flood the fellowship hall to drink champagne while the bridal party finished up photographs.

"I gotta go, Mom." She ended the call without waiting for her mother's response.

Now was her time to leave. Not just the church, but Texas. There was nothing there for her anymore. She couldn't ask Ritt to sign the papers, not with her heart still attached to him. But she couldn't stay. There was too much hurt between them.

She had a life to return to. What there was of it.

How had things gotten so messed up in such a short time?

All she could do was blame it on Texas. It did crazy stuff to her heart.

****

An hour and a half later, Shelby let herself back into the church. She had a couple of items to get, cake plates and such, then she would be on her way. She gathered her things, stacking them in plastic grocery sacks to carry them to the car.

Her phone chimed as she dropped the key into the church mailbox.

She looked at the message. Ritt.

Meet me at the Longbranch. I'll wait for you there.

That was so like him, send her a demand and expect her to comply. She had half a mind to get in her car and keep driving. She didn't owe him a thing after last night. Her phone pinged again.

Please.

Shelby sighed and texted him back. *I'm on my way.*

****

146

The Longbranch had been there as long as Shelby could remember. Half bar, half restaurant and all Texas honky tonk. Not that she had gone there much as a teenager. She and Ritt had been much more interested in places where they could be alone.

The parking lot was nearly empty when she pulled her rental car into the space by Ritt's rusty pickup. Four o'clock was an odd time, not quite the hour to drown sorrows and dreams in the beer on tap.

Shelby stepped inside and blinked several times, allowing her eyes to adjust to the dim interior.

Her gaze swept the room. Everything looked the same as she remembered. Things in Texas might be bigger, but out here, they moved at a slower pace as well. Same ol' dark paneled walls, same ol' dance floor, same ol' barkeep wiping down the bar. The blond-haired waitress was perched on a stool, flipping the pages of a glossy magazine. A sad country song drifted from the jukebox, but soon Shelby knew that the band would be warming up for their Saturday night gig.

The blonde looked up, tossing her hair over her shoulder. As she rose to her feet, Shelby pointed to the booth where Ritt sat. The waitress smiled and shot the barkeep a knowing look.

Shelby's heart pounded against her ribs as she made her way toward her husband.

He didn't glance up as she sat down.

He looked handsome and troubled. Still in his tux from the wedding, dark-blue tie hanging loose around his neck, top button undone. He rolled something between his fingers, staring at it as if it contained the answers to solving world hunger. A half-empty tumbler sat in front of him, its dark amber liquid looking wickedly potent.

"Can I get you something?" the waitress asked.

Shelby shook her head. "No. Thanks."

As if sensing they needed to be left alone, the waitress backed up a couple of steps then returned to the bar.

Ritt finally looked up, his expression guarded. "The cakes looked beautiful."

"Thanks."

"You really know your stuff."

Shelby clasped her hands in her lap, to stop their shaking. "You didn't call me here to discuss the cakes."

He pressed his lips together, then he shook his head. "No, I didn't."

He dropped what he had been holding. A paperclip. Then he slid a manila folder across the table to her. "You win. Signed them this afternoon." The divorce papers.

Shelby swallowed back tears. So much had happened in the few days that she had been in Texas. She had traveled so far to have those very papers signed and the divorce secured. Now that she had it, she didn't want it anymore. She still loved her husband with as much feeling as she had from the beginning. He was the other half of her soul, the reason she had the guts to become the woman she was today. Leaving him again would tear her heart to pieces.

"Thanks," she managed to whisper. She picked up the packet and started to scoot from the bench. She needed to get out of there before she broke down.

Ritt caught her wrist before she rose, effectively stopping her escape. "That's the new set. Craig said to be sure and have your attorney look them over before you sign."

She shouldn't have been so happy the papers didn't carry both of their signatures. It left a little room for hope. But only a little.

She adjusted the strap of her handbag and gathered her gumption to walk away. Too bad her feet didn't get the memo. "My mom called this morning."

"Oh yeah?"

"I'm sorry I didn't believe you."

He shrugged. "It doesn't matter."

It did, but there was no sense arguing about it. "Okay then," she said, lurching to her feet. "I guess I'll be seein' ya."

He nodded.

She took two steps toward the door, feeling as if her entire being was shattering to bits. Why did love have to hurt so much?

"Shelby?"

She stopped, aware that every patron in the place was studying them with unveiled interest.

"I didn't mean to hurt you. Not last night. Not ever."

She nodded. "I know." Then without another glance at his handsome face, she made her way out the door and out of Ritt's life.

Don't cry, don't cry, don't cry.

But the door handle was blurred as she reached for it. She fumbled with the unlock button on the key ring then tried again. As she finally managed to get the door open, the tears started to fall. She wiped them away with the back of one hand and tossed the manila folder onto the passenger's seat.

It was done. She got what she had set out to get: Ritt's signature on the divorce papers.

What would happen if she went back in there and told him she didn't want the divorce any longer? That she loved him and wanted them to be together forever?

150

He'd probably laugh at her. Or worse, pity her.

Blindly, she shoved the key in the ignition then took a deep shuddering breath. She had to get control for the drive back to Ritt's house. She should have thrown her bag in the car before she left the house, but she hadn't known this morning that she would want to leave. That Ritt would finally sign the papers. Car started, tears in check, Shelby turned the rental toward Randall.

At least this way she could say goodbye to Kyle. She wouldn't think about the fact that she wouldn't see him or his brother again. A thought like that would start her tears anew.

She needed to remember all the incompatibilities between her and Ritt. She lived in California now. She had built a life for herself. Though her mother had continued to travel around, moving from the Golden State to Nevada and on to Seattle, Shelby had stayed put, nurtured roots, started a business. Her life was in California.

And Ritt's life was in Texas. Just as she couldn't leave the West Coast, she couldn't ask him to leave his family...even his job at the bait shop. He was happy with his life, and she couldn't expect him to give that up.

151

It was hopeless. She could see that now. Even if he had asked her to stay, what would she do? Move her entire business to Texas?

She pushed aside the little voice that whispered, why not? Kat had wanted to buy her out for years. Shelby supposed that she could move her operation to Texas. But Ritt had signed the divorce papers. He was setting her free. The fact that Randall didn't have a bakery to speak of—unless she counted the donut shop—was a moot point; her husband didn't want her anymore.

She swallowed a sob as she pulled the rental into the driveway. Kyle's modified jeep sat next to another car. Ritt had a guest.

She put the car in park and turned off the engine. She had no idea when the next flight out of Amarillo would be, but it didn't matter. She would camp out at the airport if need be. She wasn't going to be hanging around when Ritt decided to come home.

She grabbed her purse and got out of the car as a blond woman came out of the house. Patty McCoy had gained a couple of pounds in the last few years, but Shelby would have known her anywhere.

Ritt's mother met her halfway to the house, and Shelby braced herself for whatever was to come: contempt, anger, disappointment. Patty McCoy was nothing if not her son's champion.

She opened her mouth to speak, but Shelby held up her hand to stay the words. "Don't." Her voice wavered, and she had to take a fortifying breath before continuing. "I came to get my stuff, then I'm leaving."

"You're leaving? Why?"

"Ritt signed the papers, and...it's time for me to go home." She tried to smile, but instead her mouth sort of wobbled.

"He signed the papers?"

Surely she didn't expect Shelby to say the words again. They were hard enough to get out the first time.

Shelby bit her lip and nodded.

But Patty shook her head. "Come in here and talk with me."

"I really should go," Shelby said, even as she allowed Patty to lead her into the house. "I should have never come here in the first place."

"Then why did you?" Ritt's mother turned to face her as they entered the kitchen, leaning one hip against the counter.

"He wouldn't sign them any other way." Shelby wrapped her arms around her middle. Maybe if she held on tight enough she could hold herself together until she got to California...or the airport...or maybe just back to her rental.

153

"I'm afraid I don't understand."

"I sent the papers months ago, but he refused to sign them."

"Shelby, doesn't that tell you something?"

She wanted to believe that maybe he hadn't wanted a divorce, but he had signed them now. Whatever he thought could be between them...well, it seemed he'd changed his mind after all.

"It's not like I could stay here. I have a job, a business in California. And Ritt...well, he has his work at the bait shop."

Patty shook her head. "You know why he works there? Because it's a lot like high school. There, he can pretend like you never left." She took a deep breath and leaned close, patting Shelby's arm. "I've tried to live my life the best I could. Despite that, I've made mistakes. More than I care to admit. But offering your mother money to take you away...well, it seemed like a good idea at the time. Looking back...all I can say now is I'm sorry. I hope you can forgive me."

Shelby dipped her chin and swallowed hard. "Of course I can." Tears welled in her eyes as Patty pulled her close for a hug.

Shelby squeezed her tight then stepped back, wiping the tears from her eyes. "I guess I'll get my things and be on my way."

Patty frowned. "Didn't you hear what I said? You don't need to leave."

"Yes, I do." Shelby nodded sadly.

"Ritt loves you."

"If he loves me, then why did he sign the papers?"

"Because I thought that's what you wanted." His voice came from behind her.

"Ritt?" Shelby turned as her husband came into the house, still wearing his tux from the wedding.

"Hi, Mom." He bent to kiss Patty's cheek. "I thought you said Sunday."

She shrugged. "I made your father take me to the airport in Branson. He'll be in tomorrow."

"You didn't have to do that."

But Patty nodded pointedly toward Shelby. "Yes. I did."

Ritt turned back to her. "I figured you'd be halfway to the airport by now."

Dumbly, she shook her head.

"I would have stalled her until you came home," Patty admitted. "It's seven years overdue, but it's time to clear the air."

Ritt nodded.

"What do you mean you signed the papers because that's what I wanted?"

"It's not what you want?"

Shelby pinched the bridge of her nose as her head began to pound. It wasn't what she wanted. Not anymore. But to admit that would be admitting that she still loved him. And that would leave her heart open to be broken once again.

It was a chance she had to take.

Ritt deserved the truth. After everything they had been through, that was the least she could offer him.

"No," she whispered.

"Did you sign them?"

She shook her head.

"Don't play games with me, Shel."

"I think I'll…just go…out and…see Kyle…" Patty backed toward the doorway and disappeared down the hall, leaving Shelby alone with Ritt.

"I'm not playing games." She sucked in a deep breath then raised her gaze to his. "I love you, Ritt. I always have. I didn't sign the papers because I've changed my mind. I don't want a divorce."

Instead of holding out his arms to her, he crossed them, staring down at her with those knowing blue eyes. "You didn't sign the papers, but you've obviously been reading them."

"I don't know what you're talking about." Hope stilled in her chest. She didn't know whether to cut her losses or stay and fight for the one thing she wanted most.

"What about your respectability? Your business? Your home is in California."

She shook her head. Her home had never been on the coast. Even with as much effort as she had put into her apartment, her business.

"Are you saying you're willing to stay here in Texas with me?"

She couldn't imagine him in California. Here. In Randall. That was where they both belonged. "Yes."

"I work at the bait shop."

"I know."

"And I still live with my parents."

"I don't care about that."

"Are you sure you haven't read the papers?"

"What do the papers have to do with any of this?"

He pulled the divorce papers from the inside pocket of his jacket and held them out to her. "You need to read these."

"Read them?"

He flipped through the pages until he came to what he was looking for. He folded them where she could see, then offered them to her once again.

Dread mixed with the hope in her veins as she hastily scanned the words. Then her gaze hit

157

a number and bounced back to his. "You're worth fifty-three million dollars?"

He pushed his hands into his pockets and shrugged. "Give or take."

"I don't understand."

"I invented this little doo-hickey that goes into the—well, I won't bore you with all the details, but it revolutionized the carbon black industry."

"You're saying you're rich?"

"I'm saying we're rich." Finally there was a smile on her husband's face.

"Why didn't you tell me before?"

His mouth gained a wry twist. "I was afraid that it would change how you feel about me."

She tossed the papers onto the floor and grabbed a handful of his shirt, pulling him to her. She pressed her lips to his, kissing him with all the love that she had bubbling inside. Several minutes later she ended the kiss. "Do you still think it matters to me?"

He smiled at her, love shining in his eyes. "I think I'm going to need a bit more convincing," he said. "You have a couple of years?"

Shelby laughed. "I have the rest of our lives."

Epilogue

Shelby let the sheer curtain fall back in front of the full-length, sliding-glass window. Outside the ocean gently roared as it pushed against the pristine white beach. A soft breeze stirred the palm trees planted next to the hotel and created a rustle in rhythm with the sea.

Perfect. This was all so perfect.

Ritt tipped the bellhop and put the "Do Not Disturb" sign on the door handle as he closed it behind the uniformed man. A honeymoon.

"Champagne?"

"Yes, please." Shelby let her fingers trail along the silken counterpane lying on the bed and watched her husband. She had never been so happy.

Ritt crossed the room, a champagne flute in each hand. He offered one to her with a knowing smile. "What should we drink to?"

"How about unfiled divorces?"

He raised his glass in salute and she followed along, watching him as they drank their toast. The champagne was marvelous, the best she had ever tasted. Or maybe it was the company.

She set down her glass and took a step toward him. This was their honeymoon, and she intended to make the best of it. She slipped into his arms, loving the feel of his heart so close to hers, his heat soaking through the thin cotton of her dress.

His lips captured hers in a loving kiss, a sweet prelude to what was to come. "I love you," he said, dropping another kiss on her collarbone, one at her temple and the corner of her eye.

"Tell me again."

"I love you."

She sighed as he continued his gentle onslaught to her senses. "I never get tired of hearing that."

He tilted her chin up and planted a chaste kiss on her waiting lips. "Shelby." He paused. "There's something I want to talk to you about."

"Uh-huh," she said, running her hands over the hard, warm planes of his chest.

A groan escaped him as she pressed her lips to his, one adventurous hand sliding down the front of his shirt over his belt and on to the treasure below.

"I want—" He sucked in a breath as her searching fingers found their target and cupped his warmth in her soft grasp.

"Yes," she purred as breathless with anticipation as her husband.

"I want us to try to have a baby."

The last words she expected him to say. She took a step back, not knowing how to respond, unable to find the words within her.

"It doesn't have to be right away, but soon...when you're ready. And—"

160

She didn't let him finish what he was about to say. She threw her arms around her husband, so thankful that they had found each other once again. "Yes," she whispered as happy tears filled her eyes. Who would have thought things would turn out like this? "Yes."

He pulled her hands from around his neck, grasping her fingers in his as he captured her lips in a sweet, sweet kiss.

"I can't believe this is my life—our life." She laid her head on his chest, loving the feel of him so close to her.

"Because we're millionaires?"

She tipped her hair back to meet his gaze. "Because you love me."

He chuckled, the sounds rumbling from deep within. "Having money doesn't hurt."

"No, it doesn't." It gave them one less thing to worry about.

"It didn't mean anything without you."

"And that's why you continued to live with your parents and work at the bait shop?"

Blame it on Texas

He nodded.

She smiled, running her fingers over his mouth, loving the freedom to touch him as much as she wanted. "Does this mean you're buying a new truck?"

"Absolutely not."

She reached up and kissed him again.

"Well, maybe," he said against her lips. "When the babies start coming."

She rained kisses on his face, loving the knowledge that he was hers once more. "I love you, Ritt. It took coming back to Texas and living with you again to make me realize that I'd left the best part of my life behind."

Ritt cupped her face in his hands and kissed her back. "It took you long enough."

"Oh, yeah?"

"Yeah," he said, brushing her tears away with the pads of his thumbs. "I've known this since we were nineteen."

She smiled then pressed her lips to his once again.

"It may have taken me a while, but I'm here now."

"Yes," he said. "And that's exactly where you're going to stay. Forever."

"Forever."

About the Author

Amy Lillard is the award-winning, best-selling author of over seventy books and novellas in a variety of genres.

A transplanted Southern belle, Amy was born and raised in Mississippi and now lives in Oklahoma with her husband of a billion years. They have one (almost) adult son whom they are embarrassingly proud of. These days their 'empty nest' is rounded out with two spoiled cats who always seem to want to be fed when she's hit her writing stride for the day. But such is life with felines. >^..^<

Amy loves to hear from her readers.
She can be reached at
amylillard@hotmail.com or found on the
web at www.amywritesromance.com